About the author

Jim Kjeldsen currently makes his home on the Columbia River in Vancouver, Washington. He is the author of twenty novels, mostly historical fiction.

DOCTOR JOHN

Jim Kjeldsen

DOCTOR JOHN

Vanguard Press

VANGUARD PAPERBACK

© Copyright 2024 **Jim Kjeldsen**

The right of Jim Kjeldsen to be identified as author of this work has been asserted by him in accordance with the Copyright, Designs and Patents Act 1988.

All Rights Reserved

No reproduction, copy or transmission of this publication may be made without written permission.
No paragraph of this publication may be reproduced, copied or transmitted save with the written permission of the publisher, or in accordance with the provisions of the Copyright Act 1956 (as amended).

Any person who commits any unauthorised act in relation to this publication may be liable to criminal prosecution and civil claims for damages.

A CIP catalogue record for this title is available from the British Library.

ISBN 978-1-80016-769-8

Vanguard Press is an imprint of
Pegasus Elliot Mackenzie Publishers Ltd.
www.pegasuspublishers.com

First Published in 2024

Vanguard Press
Sheraton House Castle Park
Cambridge England

Printed & Bound in Great Britain

Dedication

Special thanks to editor Don Graydon, whose assistance and insight were invaluable.

1.1

They say that I am pretty. I wouldn't know. First, I don't know what pretty means. Does it mean that I have white-woman features? I do not. Besides, I don't think many of the white women I've met are particularly attractive, although maybe they are to their horses.

Does it mean that I have native features? I don't have those, either.

Out here where I live, pretty has no meaning, there is so little to compare it to. If it means female and available, then I plead guilty. I am those things even if I don't want to be. It is what I am, and I cannot change that. As it says in the Bhagavad Gita: 'Shree Krishna grants Arjun divine vision to see his infinite form that comprises all the universes. Arjun sees the entire creation in the body of the god of gods with unlimited arms, faces, and stomachs. It has no beginning or end and extends immeasurably in all directions'.

The Bible says man was created in the image and likeness of God, and if that is so then I am Krishna, created in his image and likeness. As Voltaire said: 'Je ne suis pas d'accord avec ce que vous dites, mais je me battrai jusqu'à la mort pour que vous ayez le droit de le dire.' (I do not agree with what you have to say but I'll defend to the death your right to say it.)

Then let me have my opinions.

There is a great deal of time to think about these things where I live. Yet, this also is the cynosure of existence, the infinite form with unlimited arms, faces, and stomachs. There is no place else quite like it on the face of this Earth.

Isaac Newton's second law of motion suggests dissolution, a system running down on itself – inexorable disorder, death, and the end of the universe. My own life has had its downward spirals as well, although it was hard to tell at the time whether I was going up or down. They both may have occurred simultaneously. As the Chinese sage Lao Tzu said: 'The truth is not always beautiful, nor beautiful words the truth.'

This morning, Father is on Main Street taking his daily constitutional. I can see him from my window peering down at the falls below. He is entropy itself winding down. He wasn't always like this. At one time, he was the emperor of a vast domain – one of the largest in the world – a first among equals, with all manner of men high and low bowing to his presence. They were captivated by his power, yes, but also by his majesty, which was better than any king because father created ithimself and earned it through incredible discipline and hard work.

This is his story. I have lived it too as his daughter and can cite chapter and verse much as a sea captain would write to let his ship's owners and benefactors know what has occurred and when so they can use it for tabulating gains and losses.

I am Marie Eloisa McLoughlin Rae Harvey, born February 13, 1817, at Fort William on the Kaministiquia River on the north shore of Lake Superior. My mother was Marguerite Waden McLoughlin, the daughter of Jean-Étienne Waddens, who was born in Switzerland in 1738 and killed in an altercation with Peter Pond in March 1782 at Lac La Ronge, Canada. Peter Pond, who was a soldier with the Connecticut regiment during the French and Indian War, and Jean-Étienne Waddens, who was a soldier on the opposing French side during that same war, maintained a lucrative trade with the northern natives from Lake Athabasca. Waddens was fatally wounded in a knife fight, which was later judged to be little more than a jealous murder. However, Peter Ponds was never prosecuted for the crime.

My mother, who was seven years old at the time, and her mother both were with my grandfather when he was killed, as Jean-Étienne Waddens was a faithful husband who always traveled with his wife and child. After that, they eked out a meager existence at Lac la

Ronge, having been offered no compensation by the greedy, vainglorious, and drunken Peter Pond.

My grandmother, Oginiwaande, named for the rose color of her hair, and my mother told me a great many traditional Ojibwe stories, such as the one about *maymaygwaysiwuk*, the secretive little people who lived underwater in Lake Superior and paddled stone canoes. My mother would relate those stories to me and to the servants employed by the Hudson's Bay Company while we were at Fort Vancouver on the Columbia River.

It was in 1794 at the age of nineteen that my mother began a relationship with a Nor'West Company clerk, Alexander McKay, who was stationed at Lac la Loche. He was an expert on land-based travel and in 1793 served as lieutenant in Alexander McKenzie's historic expedition to the Pacific Ocean on behalf of the Nor'West Company. This made McKay among the very first people to cross the entire breadth of North America, and he did it nine years before Lewis and Clark's heralded expedition.

Between 1794 and 1801, Marguerite and Alexander had four children. They included three daughters – Nancy, Mary, and Catherine, all of whom were married before Marguerite went to Fort Vancouver – and one son, Thomas. In Catherine's baptismal record, her mother is not mentioned by name but instead is called 'a woman of the Indian country', which was in keeping with French tradition. Many French trappers took temporary wives among the natives and often abandoned them when they left.

In 1808, Alexander McKay resigned from the Nor'West Company and retired to Montreal. In 1810, he became a partner in the Pacific Fur Company, a newly formed American fur-trading enterprise founded by millionaire New York real estate speculator John Jacob Astor. McKay went by sea to set up a post at the mouth of the Columbia River and took his son Thomas, who was thirteen years old at the time, with him on board the ship *Tonquin*. The expedition reached the Columbia River in March 1811. That June, Alexander McKay was killed when the *Tonquin* was on a trading expedition in Nootka Sound on Vancouver Island. The *Tonquin*'s captain, the despotic Jonathan Thorne, became irritated at a Nuu-chah-nulth chief who was adept at bargaining for furs, grasped the otter skin the chief was holding, and rubbed it in his face.

The chief took it calmly, but it was a cardinal principle of native life that you never assaulted a chief. The next morning, his people swarmed the ship, pulled knives out of hiding, and stabbed to death all the crew members, including my grandfather. A crewman who was wounded crept into the powder store in the hold of the ship and set it off. The *Tonquin* was carrying extra gunpowder for trade with Russian outposts farther north, and the resulting explosion wiped out hundreds of Nuu-chah-nulth. It has been said in native records that the wailing could be heard at Lake Athabasca a thousand miles away.

My mother was not involved in this incident, although she still deeply cared for Alexander McKay even after he abandoned her. Her son and my half-brother, Thomas McKay, remained at Fort Astoria safe from harm. Thus, I grew up in a large family consisting of three half-sisters and a half-brother; a son by my father and his first wife; my older brother John Jr.; my older sister Eliza; and my younger brother David. The patriarch was my father, Doctor John McLoughlin.

To describe him fully would be to write an entire book on his history, so I will shorten the description here for the sake of brevity.

John McLoughlin (pronounced McGlocklin, with a Scottish burr), was born on October 19, 1784, in Rivière-du-Loup, Quebec. His grandfather came from County Donegal in Ireland and was of Scottish origin. All of my father's Scottish ancestors were of Irish extraction, which may account for his fiery temper. His father was John McLoughlin, a native of Ireland who went to Canada and drowned in the St. Lawrence River while John was still young. His mother's maiden name was Angelique Fraser, and she was born in Beaumont, Canada. Her father was Malcolm Ffraser, a native of Scotland and a wealthy landowner who spelled his name with two 'fs'. The McLoughlin family was poor, but they were members of the Mac Loughlins of Clan Owen, who were precursors of the first Christian king of Ireland and were very proud of it.

John McLoughlin's father and mother had seven children, five of whom were girls. He was the second child, and his brother David the third. John and David were brought up in the home of their maternal grandfather, William Fraser, after their father died. His mother, my grandmother, was the niece of Simon Fraser, the great explorer who discovered the Fraser River.

John McLoughlin was fourteen years old when he began his medical apprenticeship with Doctor James Fisher of Quebec and not yet nineteen in May 1803 when he passed the exam and was granted a license to practice medicine in Lower Canada. He always was a quick study. On April 26, 1803, he signed an agreement with McTavish, Frobisher and Company, who were partners in the Nor'West Company, to serve as a physician and apprentice clerk for five years at the paltry stipend of £20 a year. Nor'West agent Simon McTavish's promises of eventual success convinced my father to sign on. However, he was forced to leave Lower Canada due to an altercation with a British soldier.

Dr. John McLoughlin was put in charge as assistant surgeon at Fort William, which was then located at Rainy Lake. When he came to Fort

William, where I was born, he carried with him an infant son by his first wife, an Ojibwe woman who died not long after giving birth in 1809. Her name was Sah-gah-je-way-quay. Rather than pronounce that, my father called her 'Annie' after his mother. This son was Joseph, who would in time come to live with us after he received his education.

1.2

Fort William was the chief depot and fur-processing factory in 1921 when the Nor'West Company merged with the Hudson's Bay Company. By that time my father had a reputation for keeping out independent trappers, who mainly were Americans such as Peter Pond, the trapper who killed my grandfather at Lake Athabasca. Doctor John was promoted to chief factor and put in charge of the operation. It was there that he met my mother, Marguerite Waden McKay, in 1810.

At the time, he was in his late twenties and she was in her mid-thirties. Both had small children, and it was only natural that they should merge families. He was headstrong, while she was cool and collected, and they evened each other out. Although my mother could neither read nor write, and he had been educated as a physician, they got along very well, probably because she was intelligent and spoke three languages fluently – French, English, and Ojibwe – and he was tolerant of native ways.

His brother David, who also was educated as a physician, served as an apprentice surgeon in the

British army and after the Battle of Waterloo and Napoleon's defeat practiced medicine in Paris. My father joined him there for a time before entering service in the Nor'West Company. Father was a mediocre doctor by his own account, very unlike his brother, who was famed for his medical treatments in Paris and who eventually became court physician to King Louis-Philippe in France.

Doctor John, as we called him, foresaw himself as a gentleman farmer living out his days on the St. Lawrence River or as a physician in the sophisticated city of Quebec. It is evident from his letters, sent during his early years at Fort William as an assistant physician and apprentice clerk, that he planned to return to his family and make it as a doctor back in 'civilization'. His letters also reflect a distaste for frontier life, dissatisfaction with his pay and prospects, and unhappiness with the fur trade in general. He changed his mind only after he was made a chief factor and put in charge at Fort William.

Doctor John sent his three oldest children to Montreal or Quebec to be educated as soon as they were old enough. Eliza was sent to the Ursuline Convent in Montreal, where our aunt, Marie Louise McLoughlin, was mother superior of Canada's oldest and most respected girls school. The two older boys, Joseph and John Jr, went on to Europe for additional schooling. I traveled with my younger brother David and with our parents to Oregon when he was three years old and I was seven.

It says a great deal about my father's attitude toward native nations and his aptitude for dealing with tribal peoples that he permitted us to accompany him on this 2,500-mile overland journey across the continent. He felt it was an essential part of our education, and he intensely disliked the thought of being away from his family. He'd already been away for lengthy periods of time, the last of which was when I was born, when he went to London to negotiate the merger of the Nor'West Company and the Hudson's Bay Company.

In the end, Doctor John felt that the Nor'Westers gave up too much for the sake of peace in order to quell the fighting between the two companies, and in the end he was proven to be correct. The Nor'West Company virtually disappeared within a few years after the merger, leaving behind only a trace of itself. The Hudson's Bay Company assumed pre-eminence with its strict hierarchical and aristocratic bearings.

In 1821 father was named one of the chief factors of the new company and assigned to his old post at Rainy Lake. There he carried on a brisk competition with American fur traders who were continually pushing north across the boundary, and it ultimately was this success that prompted Hudson's Bay Company Superintendent George Simpson to choose him in 1824 as the new head of the Columbia District, where even more competition from the intrusive and uncooperative Americans was expected. The Northwest at the time was under the dual governorship of the British and the Americans, but nobody was really in charge, and law and order was left up to the Hudson's Bay Company, a private enterprise.

Simpson, as the newly appointed governor-in-chief locum tenens, with typical bravado decided to

go to Fort William himself for the announcement that Doctor John would be taking over. There, on May 28, 1824, he and my father met for the first time. This encounter was to be of great significance given the policy that would be pursued in the Columbia District, that huge area west of the Rockies centering on the valleys of the Columbia River and its tributaries in which the Nor'West Company had been active since 1813. Returns had been disappointing, and Simpson had already decided that a change of command was necessary. The chief factor, John Dugald Cameron, was transferred to Rainy Lake, and Doctor John was assigned to Fort George on the Columbia River, which was at that time was the district depot.

While they were at Fort William, our family lived in the surgery and apothecary building near the fort gate. What they encountered at Fort George was unlike anything they'd experienced before, and it took a while to adapt to it.

Corporate turbulence already had caused a lot of drama in the McLoughlin household. In 1816, Doctor John, along with the other Nor'West Company partners at Fort William, was arrested by the Hudson's Bay Company under suspicion that they'd instigated an attack on Bay men and settlers at the Battle of Seven Oaks in the Red River colony. While my father awaited trial in Montreal, Marguerite spent the winter of 1816-17 alone at Fort William pregnant with me. She was also alone for my birth that February.

My father's trial was delayed, and he was able to return to Fort William that summer. The trial was rescheduled to 1818, when Marguerite was left alone with the children again, this time for over a year. He ultimately was acquitted of all charges after testimony indicated that he had nothing to do with the attack.

His had been one of a Nor'West Company party that arrived late at the Red River settlement in June 1816, thereby avoiding any active part in the massacre at Seven Oaks. Outraged, Thomas Douglas, the fifth earl of Selkirk, nevertheless promptly led his private mercenaries to the Nor'West Company at Fort William and arrested the trading partners. The indicted party traveled to the trial by canoe, which was swamped in Lake Superior. Nine men drowned, and my father was dragged unconscious and barely alive from the water. The experience turned his formerly thick shock of blond hair snow white even though he was only thirty-two years old. He was not clear of the ensuing legal entanglements until he was found not guilty in October 1818, and from there went straight to England to mediate the merger of the two companies.

On July 27, 1824, after just two weeks of preparation, my father and mother bundled up me and my brother David and left Fort William for our new home, traveling overland with a retinue of Bay personnel for protection. We were in a whip buggy drawn by two horses and made what I regarded as spectacular time.

Nevertheless, twenty days later just beyond Lac la Biche a little short of the Athabasca River, George Simpson joined our party. He left York Factory on the shores of Hudson's Bay accompanied by an aide on August 15, 1824, in a canoe manned by eight men and a native guide. The journal he kept reflects his passion for speed. Six weeks after leaving York Factory, Simpson overtook us, and we arrived at Fort George together on November 8, ending Simpson's journey of eighty-four days – twenty fewer than the previous record from Hudson's Bay to the Pacific.

Yet, there was more to it than that. Whereas my father came from a distinguished ancestry, George Simpson was born out of wedlock. In those days, when heritage meant everything, he was commonly referred to as a bastard. In addition, due to my father's Herculean dimensions, he towered over Simpson, who at five-feet-seven was a full head shorter. Both men were muscular and powerfully built, but my father projected an overwhelming aura of physical strength. With his mane of white hair and fierce demeanor, standing next to him Simpson looked like a country rube. Known as the 'little emperor' for his Napoleonic demeanor as well as for his diminutive stature, he would in subsequent years travel constantly by canoe and horseback back and forth across the continent. It seemed to be a point of manliness with him, and he decidedly needed to be manly standing next to my father.

Simpson kept a book of notes, his 'Character Book', a clandestine record of more than 150 Bay people under his command. He recorded no names but instead used a numbering system. In this book, based on their meeting at Lac la Biche, he described my father as 'such a figure as I should not like to meet on a dark night in one of the bye lanes in the neighborhood of London. Dressed in clothes that had once been fashionable but were now covered with a thousand patches of different colors, the beard would do honor to the chin of a grizzly bear, his face and hands evidently show that he had not lost much time at his toilette. He was loaded with arms and his own Herculean dimensions formed a tout ensemble that would convey a good idea of the highwaymen of former days. He was ungovernable, with a violent temper and turbulent disposition'.

The Hudson's Bay Company domain my father was given to govern encompassed almost six million square miles, equivalent to most of Europe and about a twelfth of the earth's surface. George Simpson was sage enough to realize that it took a potent personage to rule over such a domain. Even so, he resented my father. Ever polite, I could nonetheless see it in his eyes as he surveyed us on that monumental trip. I knew then that nothing but ill would come to pass between them.

The combined party reached an HBC trading post just short of the Rocky Mountains in October, and my half-brother Thomas McKay was waiting there with horses and men to help us across the Rockies. He had grown up in the fur trade and become a well-regarded clerk and trader for the Bay. This was the first time he had seen our mother since leaving for Fort Astoria with his father thirteen years before. It was a most tender reunion, and one that George Simpson derided as unmanly. One did not, after all, submit to women, not even to one's own mother.

Yet, tall, dark and fearsome, and a better shot than Natty Bumppo was in the fictional 'Leatherstocking Tales' of James Fenimore Cooper, Thomas was held in awe by the natives, much as Natty Bumppo had been in the novel. Except, this was no novel. It was real life. Thomas was tall, muscular, had a thin face, black hair, and restless black eyes set beneath projecting eyebrows. He worked as a clerk, interpreter, and guide for various fur companies. After retiring in 1839, he spent his remaining years between his farm at Champoeg and his farm at Scappoose in Oregon. His daughters stayed at the Whitman Mission near Walla Walla to obtain an education.

1.3

On October 27, 1824, eight days after my father's 40th birthday, the assemblage of travelers came to where the Spokane River flows into the Columbia north of Walla Walla and found Peter Ogden waiting for them along with thirty voyagers. Ogden had decided to wait for the party in case Simpson wanted to make a side trip to Spokan House nearby. He was a key figure in Simpson's plan for the famed Snake River brigade of wandering trappers, a strategy designed to keep Americans out of the area.

What Ogden faced was daunting. An example was Antoine Benoit, who in 1824 joined Ogden's Snake brigade as a freeman trapper and on April 8, 1825, was leading some horses when he was surrounded by Blackfoots and shot and stabbed to death. The natives took his three horses and sixteen beaver skins. His body was recovered naked, the scalp taken, a ball in the body, one in the head, and three stab wounds with a knife. He could not have suffered long. He was buried on the east bank of the Snake River in a beaver dam.

Ogden had two native wives and treated them both respectfully. His father, Isaac Ogden, was a judge in Montreal. In 1811 when Ogden was seventeen, he joined the Nor'West Company, was stationed at Isle la Crosse, and married a Cree woman. When he was twenty-four he came down the Columbia to Astoria, where for a year or two he was in charge of trapping parties operating between the mouth of the Columbia and Puget Sound. In 1821, the companies merged, and in spring 1824 Ogden was appointed chief trader.

After the death of his first wife, Ogden married a woman from the Spokan tribe. Ogden traveled, explored, and trapped an area covering Oregon, Idaho, parts of California, Nevada, Utah, and Wyoming. The geography of the Snake country was a bewildering puzzle of different watersheds and drainage areas, with rumors of westward-flowing rivers and inland seas that did not exist. Ogden beganto untangle the maze and by 1830 had a better knowledge of the area than any other explorer.

Upon his arrival at the mouth of the Spokane River, Simpson sacked Fort Spokan's chief trader, Alexander Ross, on the spot as lackadaisical and treasonous, noting that his reports 'are so full of bombast and marvelous nonsense that it is impossible to get any information that can be depended on from him'. Also, an inexcusable sin in Simpson's eyes was that Ross had befriended American trapper Jedediah Smith, who Simpson saw as a mortal enemy.

Ross, who by that time had grown quite corpulent, went on to become a schoolteacher, which was perhaps a life better suited for him. Ogden in his stead was given the job of trapping out the Oregon country and making a virtual fur desert of it, thereby keeping out the Americans, especially Jedediah Smith.

1.4

Our combined party arrived at Fort George on November 8, 1824. As we canoed down the Columbia River from Walla Walla the fort peeked out from the mist and trees. It was nothing more than a log stockade surrounding a rude clutch of cabins, and even the natives who traded there did not think it was very impressive. My father's initial impression of his new domain was not good.

'I cannot say that I admire much this country,' he wrote in a letter to his uncle on March 15, 1825. 'The climate is very mild, but moist and cloudy to a degree indeed since my arrival on the 8th November we have not seen one clear sun shining day and not ten days without rain'.

George Simpson, whether due to his travel addiction or a love of gloomy places, was to visit the Columbia four times, in 1824, 1829, 1836, and 1841.

During that first four months, he and my father developed plans that enabled the company to take the offensive against both the Russians, who were trading up the coast, and the Americans, who were in their midst, and eventually dominate the fur trade from the Columbia all the way up to Alaska. Simpson, who was absolutely convinced that the Fraser River was a superior outlet for furs from the interior than the Columbia River, sent James McMillan north to establish Fort Langley on the lower Fraser and coordinate Langley as the central locus of the region in place of Fort George.

Simon Fraser had explored the river and declared it unnavigable. Simpson wanted to prove him wrong, and four years later on a canoe trip down the river nearly lost his life in doing so. Not only did the river flood wildly during winter snowmelts, it shot through narrow canyons with cliffs on either side so steep that only a few footpaths could be carved out. These were not accessible even by donkey. Simon Fraser was right after all, and Simpson turned Fort Langley into an agricultural depot that provided the Hudson's Bay Company and Russian posts with meat and produce. Although forced by circumstance to give in, Simpson highly resented the fact that Doctor John's great-uncle Simon Fraser could not be proven wrong, and he held it against my father.

Simpson, in all respects, was that kind of a man.

1.5

Fort George was a log stockade surrounded by immensely tall and thick evergreen trees. To create the clearing in the first place required a saw team of four men to cut through each tree, one two-man team spelling the other at intervals, and even at that it took them four days to cut through a single tree.

The cabins within the stockade were made from this timber and after more than ten years showed no sign of deterioration the wood was so strong and the grain so tight.

Fine as the wood was, the huts had been built in haste and without energy, slapped together on the fly as the workers were engaged in other tasks. The natives who traded there exchanged furs for goods through a small door at the stockade entrance and, peering inside, found absolutely nothing in the fort that was impressive. Their own village longhouses were much more luxurious and well-built. They coveted the axes and cook pots the Bay offered, and their wives grabbed ceaselessly at the beads and other ornaments the company provided, so they'd come to expect opulence from the whites. But that was not the case with Fort George.

The natives marveled over these things – not the goods, because they were used to that, but the fact that the trading company would take furs in trade at all. These were not considered luxuries but commonplace items in their homes that warmed their beds and were even used as bums wipes by their chiefs and tossed away.

At Fort Walla Walla, we'd surrendered our horses and taken canoes downriver since it was a great deal faster than the five-day overland route along meandering paths. Even the canoe journey was a momentous undertaking. Gouging the Columbia Plateau and cutting through the Cascade Range as it descended the river created a series of waterfalls, rapids, and canyons.

The first, the grand rapids at Umatilla, was a long and extremely dangerous sluice at the foot of high cliffs descending seven miles to the mouth of the Umatilla River. Then came the John Day River, named after a member of the Astorian overland party who while descending the river in April 1812 was robbed and stripped naked at the mouth of the river, forcing him and his partner to hike more than eighty miles to friendly natives, where they were clothed and rescued.

His partner, Ramsay Crooks, was a Scotsman who emigrated to North America in 1803 at the age of sixteen. In 1810, he joined John Jacob Astor's Pacific Fur Company and came to Fort George overland. Ramsay and John Day fell behind the main party in the Snake River country in the winter of 1811-12. They had terrible experiences but eventually got through the snow of the Blue Mountains and fell in with friendly Walla Wallas. They were directed down the Columbia to meet their companions, and in the vicinity of the mouth of what is now the John Day River the men were met by hostile natives who robbed them of all they had, including their clothes. They were rescued when they met Robert Stuart's party descending to the Columbia. After the Pacific Fur Company was sold, Ramsay remained as Astor's employee and became a successful American entrepreneur.

Three miles below the mouth of the John Day was the Chutes, a short narrows a mile long and 250 yards wide around which our canoes had to be portaged, it being too dangerous to descend in them. Bands of native men took up the canoes, and our baggage and carried them around the difficult passages while we went on foot. These men were used to this, and in fact their families had been doing it for thousands of years for travelers who passed that way. The area was a renowned neutral zone where attacks by opposing bands were not permitted, which made the depredations at the mouth of the John Day all the more horrendous. It was said that the natives who attacked them were not at all sure whether John Day and Ramsay Crooks were even human beings since they had never seen anyone like them before.

As we entered the fort on that Monday, our path was lit by the campfires of natives who had convened there as a convenient waypoint on their travels up the river. We were greeted by them politely but with a certain amount of indifference since our mother, Marguerite, was half Ojibwe. To them, she was just another native among the many who visited the region, whether out of trade or just because they were curious. We children were regarded as possible slaves since we had rounded heads, which among the Chinook signified a lesser social position.

The one person among us who was not treated with indifference was Doctor John. He was gruff, and even insolent at times, but he was never again compared to a highwayman. That description was from Simpson, whose motives were suspect. Doctor John was a giant of a man, dignified and of courtly manner. His hair, prematurely gray but thick and bushy, framed a mobile face. His eyes were kindly but could grow icy or flash with temper, which he displayed on more than one occasion. To the natives, he was *hyas tyee*, a good chief. The key word was chief, because they held their chiefs in reverence.

From that first day, Doctor John was held in awe by the local natives. He was not only a doctor – a shaman to them – but a particularly impressive one.

To many of the natives who lived at the mouth of the Columbia, Doctor John looked like the Jehovah they'd heard about from the sailors and preachers who came off their boats in droves every time they landed at the mouth of the river.

Doctor John was six feet six inches tall – seven feet tall when he donned his beaver hat. He was almost perfectly proportioned, brave and fearless, and scorned to lie – all personality characteristics that the Chinooks greatly admired. He was heavily boned, the brows above his blue-gray eyes massive, his hair was thick, and his complexion was ruddy. His expression was habitually grave and he moved with a slow dignity that impressed the natives, who expected such demeanor from their chiefs. This was no accident. Doctor John cultivated his image carefully, patterning it after the local native chiefs.

1.6

During the Hudson's Bay Company era, Doctor John presided like a feudal king over an area larger than Alaska, more than twice the size of Texas, and seven times as large as Great Britain. By the time Fort Vancouver was built, the natives of the lower Columbia had been trading for thirty-three years with the whites, including fifteen years of those at Fort George.

When Lewis and Clark's Corps of Discovery passed through the area in 1805 it encountered one of the largest populations north of Mexico, totaling almost 5,000 Chinooks, which doubled to nearly 10,000 people during spring salmon runs. The salmon and rich river resources attracted both riverine and inland peoples, including Chinook, Cowlitz, Klikitat, Taidnapam, Shahala, Kalapuya, and Molala.

The Chinook chief Os-wal-licks, called Comcomly by the whites, dominated the fur trade. The Chinooks were keen traders, and nearly all of the furs passed through their hands. They were so tenacious in this monopoly that they would without hesitation murder any strangers who challenged their hegemony. In an attempt to deter others from visiting the fort, the Chinooks spread stories that the intruding traders were cannibals who would eat the natives alive if they had the chance.

Comcomly was described by author Washington Irving, who wrote the history of Astoria, as 'a shrewd old savage, with but one eye', but highly skilled in trade and diplomacy. He was friendly to the British and Euro-American explorers he encountered, including captains Robert Gray and George Vancouver, and received peace medals from Lewis and Clark. He also assisted the Pacific Fur Company and offered to help the Americans fight the British in the War of 1812. Instead, Astoria was sold to the British, although Comcomly was friendly with the British as well. He was entertained at Fort Vancouver by Doctor John and often piloted Hudson's Bay Company ships up the Columbia River. Comcomly died in 1830 when a fever epidemic struck his tribe. His remains were interred in a canoe in the family burial ground.

There were three main chiefs on the lower Columbia. They included Comcomly, the chief at Point George; his son Casseno, chief of the tribe opposite the river from the plain where Fort Vancouver was located; and Scanewa, the Cowlitz chief whose range went from the shores of Puget Sound to the Columbia River near Fort Vancouver.

However, the one who handled the vast majority of furs was Comcomly, and those were mostly otter furs.

The otter hunters in Kamchatka, hardened by years of harsh life and interminable winters, saw the otter as their ticket to a life of ease and went raging among the animals without discipline or order, clubbing them, drowning them, and stabbing them until large groups disappeared. The hunting became a vicious slaughter as they moved from island to island, attacking and enslaving native hunters and engaging in the massive killing of sea otters. One Russian expedition in 1768 returned with 40,000 seals and 2,000 sea otter pelts, 15,000 pounds of walrus ivory, and vast quantities of whalebone, leaving behind a wide path of death and destruction.

The region that was covered by the Hudson's Bay Company during that time also was home to ten million beaver. It contained nearly half the world's supply of fresh water, was swampy, featured innumerable lakes and ponds, and was covered with aspen and birch, which provided prime beaver food. Without a doubt, it was one of the greatest beaver habitats the world has ever known.

In the early 1800s beaver furs were in high demand in Europe, especially for men's hats, and trappers began to work inland along the rivers. The Nor'West Company opened its Spokan trading post in 1810 seeking to claim the territory before competitors arrived. The following year, David Thompson of the

Nor'West Company reached the Columbia River at Kettle Falls and began to travel downstream. On July 13, 1811, the party camped near Point Vancouver, which had been named and mapped by William Broughton in 1792 during Captain George Vancouver's survey of the Columbia. Two days later, Thompson discovered to his eternal dismay that he was a couple of months too late. Americans employed by the Pacific Fur Company had already established a trading post at Fort Astoria – later renamed Fort George – on the south side of the river and claimed that area for the United States.

Native peoples had lived on the lower Columbia River for 10,000 years before whites arrived. The natives possessed a sprawling and highly successful trade network well before Fort Vancouver was constructed in 1825. Hiring Chinook and Cowlitz in their traditional roles as middlemen, the company gained access to a spectrum of tribal trading partners that extended many hundreds of miles from the fort. The Chinook and Cowlitz were enthusiastic participants in this arrangement, which served to augment the existing wealth and importance of the lower Columbian social order.

Comcomly already was king of the clan in 1805 when Meriwether Lewis and William Clark arrived. The explorers felt they were in the wilderness beyond the pall of civilization during their journey across the country. That is, until they got to The Dalles, where the Columbia rippled across a series of shallow rocks. In French, the dalles means shallow rocks. There they got the shock of their lives. A native guide dropped something in camp and exclaimed, 'Son of a bitch!' To which the puritanical Meriwether Lewis yelped, 'What?'

'I dropped the goddamned thing,' the guide said in perfectly fluent English.

Lewis thought he might have another Squanto on his hands, the Patuxet native of Massachusetts who was kidnapped by the British and educated in England and who returned to help the Puritans survive. That was not the case. Almost all the Columbia natives knew these words, which had been picked up from American sailors who had been frequenting the mouth of the Columbia for decades. As the Lewis and Clark expedition traveled downriver, it constantly encountered trade goods from the east, including a sailor's jacket from a British ship and horse-riding boots from California.

When the American Robert Gray entered the Columbia River in 1792, Comcomly was a young man in his mid-twenties and was on hand to greet him, something that Gray seldom mentioned since he didn't want it to appear back home in Boston that the Columbia had already been claimed. After that, Comcomly took it upon himself to personally greet each incoming ship, lavishing the captains with gifts and winning their favor.

Therefore, he and other Chinooks were not at all surprised when a ragged party of some thirty white men plus a Plains woman, her baby, and a black slave hove into view in November 1805. What was bizarre was that they came down the river from the interior rather than from the sea. Why the expedition wanted to brave the Rocky Mountains was beyond Comcomly's comprehension. His own people did it regularly to hunt buffalo, and they knew there was nothing on the other side but a vast sea of grass. Just as the Chinooks had no desire to go out onto the open sea, they had no desire to sail across the inland sea.

Comcomly of course knew all about Lewis and Clark well before meeting them, having received messages about some strange people coming their way. His village was the metropolis of the north and already was chock-full of the beads, kettles, and metal gizmos that the traders thought the natives yearned for. The Chinook disdained the trade goods that Lewis and Clark carried with them. What they wanted were blankets and guns, the items that the sea captains furnished them.

Lewis and Clark somehow managed to offend the Chinooks, and their supply of salmon was temporarily cut off. Expedition members had to hunt for game and settled on elk as the most providential resource. That was a minor inconvenience, although they griped about it in their journals. What really got to them were the fleas. They were everywhere and in everything. The natives knew that fleas could not tolerate a diet of raw meat, and they chewed raw meat for this reason. What the fleas were looking for was sugary blood such as the explorers had, who imbibed all manner of sweet things and therefore caused fleas to mob them. The Chinook also knew that fleas are attracted to animals with strong odors and unhealthy skin, and their salmon diet kept them safe from that. By and large, the explorers disliked eating salmon and preferred cooked meat.

Fresh salmon averaged about ten pounds each and had to be split and dried, and these bardeaux (shingles), averaging a pound or so each, had 'little more substance than a piece of rotten wood', noted Bay clerk Frank Ermatinger. Before being cooked, the strips had to be soaked for a considerable amount of time in water, which Ermatinger termed the 'misery of damned dried salmon'.

Another thing that got to Lewis and Clark were the high-born Chinooks characterized by flat foreheads and pointed craniums, the result of head-flattening as infants. The inland Salish, who came to the Columbia to trade, were called Flatheads by French fur traders in the Nor'West Company by mistake, even though the Salish heartily disdained such practices, which they considered barbaric. Lewis and Clark perpetuated this mistake and carried it back with them.

Clark brought his personal slave, York, along on the trip, which was something the Chinooks understood. One of their most important trade items was slaves from California, along with Nuu-chah-nulth canoes from Nootka Sound, and dentalium seashells, highly valued as hair and clothing ornaments. The Chinook took slaves as captives in warfare and used them to practice thievery, which their masters refrained from as unworthy of their high status. As a result, Lewis and Clark were plagued by fleas and thievery.

What Lewis and Clark were not plagued with, despite their journal entries, was isolation. They fully expected an American ship to come into the mouth of the Columbia at any time and take them back home. Expedition members were sorely disappointed when it was decided that they would have to walk back instead.

1.7

In the days after my brother and I arrived at Fort George, we were kept inside the dismal stockade for fear that the natives would seize us and put us to work as slaves on their behalf because we had rounded heads. However, the day after we arrived we were treated to a display that few outsiders are ever likely to encounter. Comcomly, as chief of a trading empire that stretched north to the Aleutian Islands, west to the Great Lakes, and south into Alta California, was a master of social relations and myth-mongering. He knew how to put on a good show.

When we peeked outside the front gate the next morning, the entrance had been cleared of wigwam huts made of branches and wattle. The area leading down to the water was open, and on the ground were countless beaver pelts and otter hides. Stepping off a great war canoe paddled by fifty warriors came Comcomly, displaying great solemnity and dignity, on either side of him a row of 300 slaves bowing and prostrating themselves in honor of his presence. He was accompanied by several of his wives and children, along with fierce bodyguards who would stab anyone who got too close. Comcomly came inside the stockade, the only native allowed to do so, and proceeded to talk in an ordinary manner about totally mundane subjects.

This demonstration helped inspire loyalty among his people as well as among the company's officers, who were very impressed, thus ensuring expansion of his influence. It was in the company's interest to have these leaders maintaining positions of great prominence, and Comcomly knew it.

It was this show of bravado that led my father to concoct the scheme that permitted us to stay with these people and join their community. A few years later, when disease winnowed the native population down to a mere ten percent of what it had been, Doctor John found himself in the position of being the lone king of the domain who ruled by virtue of being the last man standing. He took it in stride and did almost exactly as Comcomly had done. His actions made a fortune for the Hudson's Bay Company and changed the nature of our relationships with the natives in the process.

1.8

The galvanizing force behind the Nor'West Company had been the opportunities it gave to talented traders to rise out of the ranks of salaried clerks and become wintering partners in charge of major fur-producing districts. Because wintering partners shared in the company's profits, they were aggressive about maintaining those profits. But the Nor'West Company's advance across the Rockies only worsened its economic difficulties, stretching out its supply line to 3,000 miles.

Its merger with the Hudson's Bay company probably saved both companies from bankruptcy, but unfortunately the merger retained only the outlines of the old system. Negotiators like Doctor John fought virulently for equal terms, but they were at a great disadvantage. They had to rely on Hudson's Bay Company's promises, and it simply did not keep them. Not with someone like George Simpson in charge.

The Bay's tightly knit hierarchical organization was its guarantee that the company could maintain order in the wilderness, and the British tradition of strict levels of socializing between officers and servants was continued, and its officers were by definition gentlemen, with the requisite education and social status. A typical career was to enter the company as an apprentice clerk at age sixteen, rise steadily to chief trader in charge of a post or fort, then be made chief factor of a department containing a number of posts.

The Hudson's Bay Company was managed from London, and ultimately was responsible only to a very tiny group of British shareholders who selected a governor to act on their behalf. Many backers were influential men linked to political power, yet the company was not an official agent of the crown. The goal was private profit, not extension of British sovereignty, while the Nor'West Company had been a loose partnership of equals, many allied by blood or marriage, who shared in the annual profits.

After the merger, in order to increase returns, Bay traders adopted a credit system that kept natives forever in debt to the company. Natives not only became dependent on the trading posts for goods essential to their living but for foodstuffs as well. In time, the living leveled off to a subsistence standard and the natives became virtual wards of the Hudson's Bay Company.

1.9

From the very moment he saw Fort George, George Simpson hated it. The stockade, its bastions with eighteen-pound cannons, and the complex of warehouses, shops, and dormitories, struck him as far too elaborate for a country trading post. 'Everything to me appears on the Columbia on too extended a scale except the trade', he wrote.

From John Jacob Astor's time to when he took charge, Simpson estimated that the entire return from Fort George amounted to only 20,000 beaver and otter pelts. Also, Fort George was an expensive place to maintain. The post's Pacific Coast location meant it had to be supplied by ships that traveled around Cape Horn to Hawaii before making the crossing to the Columbia bar, one of the most dangerous places in the world for ships. At times, sailing ships had to wait months before conditions were right for crossing the bar.

Most rivers form deltas at their mouths composed of sand and silt brought down from inland waters. Not the Columbia. Its mouth shot straight into the depths of the Pacific off an underwater cliff high enough to form the side of a mountain. Two miles off the entrance were towering waves breaking over the river bar. Churning waters dense with sand made soundings impossible. Sand accumulated on either side of the mouth, but only shifting sand gathered at the entrance, piling up for a time before sluicing off into the sea. No matter how often a captain visited the bar, he found it totally different from the last time. Seasoned river pilots who knew the shoals had to be taken on board to guide the ships through the maze into the river. The natives in their canoes found this to be no big deal since all they had to do was paddle a little harder. But barques, brigantines, and full-rigged sailing ships had a difficult time not scraping the bottom, or worse, breaking up in the pounding surf.

Then there was the fact that the Nor'West Company let the traders at Astoria abuse their privileges and order whatever they wanted from England. Ships making the five-month voyage around the tip of South America brought things like full suits of mail, ostrich feathers, and luxurious European provisions, all imported at enormous expense. This factored into George Simpson's assessment.

In August 1821 he ordered a full inspection of Nor'West Company posts west of the Rocky Mountains. Many of the posts could be made profitable by eliminating personnel, but the Columbia post was of strategic importance as a buffer to keeping Americans out of the richer fur areas to the north, and in 1824 Simpson was instructed by the London committee to visit the area and institute measures of economy and efficiency. He slashed the workforce by nearly half and ordered a drastic reduction in European 'eatables, drinkables, and other domestic comforts', telling his agents they could live off the land or go hungry.

The first step in making money, Simpson preached like it was his religion, was not wasting it on frivolous extravagances. It got so bad that he even tried to curtail the amount of tea each chief factor consumed, which utensils should be used at dinner (tin plates), and how tables should be set (no tablecloths or wine glasses – too expensive). However, there was another overriding factor in his decision to scuttle the old fort and relocate it upstream. Fort George was on the south side of the river. On that side, the British figured America would lay its claim of sovereignty since a fort had already been established there.

Simpson did not like Americans. He found them undisciplined, weak, and slovenly. He claimed they didn't tether their horses at night in camp but let them roam free. They were boisterous and got drunk often, that is, when they weren't being obstreperous just because they were Americans. To Simpson, it was a land in which anything went and the American system of voting smacked of anarchy. In the British tradition, orders came from on high and were obeyed without question. To do anything else was treasonous.

As time went on and my father became more like the American settlers in the Oregon country, Simpson grew to dislike him all the more intensely. Simpson believed in revenge to the fullest. He wanted to see his enemies devastated, crushed, annihilated, destroyed. Getting even wasn't enough. Doctor John came to be concluded in Simpson's list of enemies, while Doctor John himself saw no reason why beating an opponent meant his annihilation at any cost.

In their search for a north-bank post for a new fort, Doctor John was accompanied by Alexander Kennedy as they paddled together in a canoe propelled by natives. Just above the mouth of the Willamette River, at a place called Jolie Prairie by French voyageurs, they found a cut in the forest about three miles long and a mile wide. The land was relatively level, had been kept clear through a long history of burning, and had been made very fertile by the combined effects of fire ashes and copious rainfall. With its verdant fields and southern exposure, the site had agricultural potential unsurpassed along the entire lower river.

The site also had access to deep water for mooring ships and was basically immune from attack since any ships that crossed the bar and headed up the river would be reported long before they arrived. The forest was so dense and impenetrable that there could be no attack by land. The few paths that were open from Puget Sound were controlled by the natives.

There were two reasons for centering farming operations at that site. First, produce could be shipped through Puget Sound without having to make the hazardous crossing of the Columbia bar. Second, extensive agricultural operations would give England a legitimate claim to that side of the river. The British wanted the boundary with Canada to be along the Columbia River, running down the Rocky Mountains from the 49th parallel and from there out to sea, rather than the Americans insistence that it cut straight across the 49th parallel to the sea.

The bluff that Doctor John and Kennedy chose for Fort Vancouver overlooked the river and was 'sublimely grand', said David Douglas, a British botanist who visited there in 1825. It had a vista of the river and the valley, mountains covered in perpetual snow, eight-foot-tall stalks of wild lupine on the prairie, blue scilla on the riverbanks, and blooming salal with shiny leaves touching the shadowed edges of the forest – all of which were not particularly gratifying to Simpson. But the fertile soil for cultivation was.

Aemilius Simpson, George Simpson's cousin and superintendent of the marine department, bet David Douglas, the visiting botanist, £5 against an old pair of boots that he could beat him in a half-mile footrace along the edge of a bluff and back. Everyone lined up to cheer the race, which Aemilius Simpson won. He died in Alaska from one of the many liver ailments that plagued nineteenth-century seamen.

George Simpson named the fort after Captain George Vancouver, whose explorations in 1757 and 1798 helped the British lay claim to the Oregon country, even though Vancouver missed the mouth of the river entirely before American Robert Gray sailed into it. Work on the new post began immediately and proceeded through the winter of 1825. At sunrise on March 19, 1825, Simpson presided over a flag-raising ceremony, breaking the neck of a bottle of rum over the flagstaff and christening the place Fort Vancouver in honor of King George IV.

'The object is to identify our claim to the soil and to trade with Vancouver's discovery of the river and coast on behalf of Great Britain', he proclaimed to a host of native dignitaries who hadn't the slightest idea of what he was saying. The language of the region was *Chinuk wawa*, or Chinook Jargon, and Simpson didn't know a word of it.

By way of contrast, four months after our family's arrival at Fort George, my brother and I were babbling gleefully in *Chinuk wawa*, which contained about 800 words and no grammar to speak of. You just said whatever came to mind. We were *cheechakos*, or newcomers, who had arrived *skookum*, though strong water, and many native things were *cultus*, taboo, to us. I was a *klootchman* (female child), who had a great deal of *moolah*, money, given to me by *muckamucks*, or higher-ups, and so forth.

Fort Vancouver faced one problem, and that was the Columbia River itself. In front of the fort, the river was about a mile wide in the summer, but in spring it was much wider, rising as much as twenty feet higher by late spring as a result of mountain snowmelt. The floodwaters left behind huge pools of stagnant water that were ideal breeding grounds for mosquitoes. They brought the 'dreadful visitation', 'remittent fever', or 'cold sick' that struck the lower Columbia every year. This occurred in the spring and fall, and Bay men suffered less with each successive attack, although the natives did not. They died instead, having no natural resistance to malaria, smallpox, measles, diphtheria, and an overwhelming array of European diseases.

If the native who said 'son of a bitch' had been Squanto, he could have told the Bay traders that the East Coast initially was so crowded that passing British ships couldn't find a place to land since there were so many campfires burning. When the ships did land, the sailors left behind a token of their presence – disease – which spread like wildfire so the next time they came all they found were piles of skeletons. Two hundred years later, the same thing was happening on the lower Columbia.

The Nor'West company had a more egalitarian and decentralized management style than the Hudson's Bay Company. Nor'West employees freely intermarried with native women and thereby made inroads into native communities. When the Bay absorbed the Nor'West Company, it inherited the legacy of the company's relationships with the tribes. During their brief time in the region, Nor'Westers maintained positive relationships with bands throughout the country, including coastal groups as well as tribes such as the Yakama who controlled access to the interior. You came and went only if they allowed you to.

2.1

What especially terrified Hudson's Bay Company men was New Caledonia. They detested the hard duties and still harder fare of the district. In 1828, John Work wrote to ex-servant Edward Ermatinger a letter still in company archives to tell him he was glad to hear that his brother, Frank Ermatinger, had escaped New Caledonia, with its eternal solitude, through transfer. New Caledonia servants who did not desert their posts commonly quit the company rather than serve another term in the district. The living conditions were so primitive that some servants were sent there as a disciplinary measure.

Killings and drownings blackened New Caledonia's reputation. The most notorious homicide occurred in August 1823 when Joseph Bagnoit and Belone Duplantes were left in charge of Fort George by clerk James Yale while he visited Stuart Lake. They were murdered in their beds by a native and the post was pillaged. The bodies were subsequently ravaged by wild dogs and the fort was temporarily abandoned. It took four months for the voyage to and return from northern Caledonia, by boat from Fort Vancouver to Okanogan, and by horse brigade – 250 to 300 animals to a train – from Okanogan to Kamloops. Many animals died from the rigors of the trip over the winding mountain trails.

By contrast, Fort Vancouver was a haven for those who had lived in roofless camps on trapping expeditions and kept nightlong watches against marauding natives. Fort Vancouver was astonishingly cosmopolitan, with Delaware, Iroquois, Chinook slaves with normal heads, Chinook dignitaries whose sloped skulls proclaimed their superior caste, and sightseeing chieftains from the interior, Kanakas from the Sandwich Islands, Metis from Assiniboine, Canadian artisans from Manchester or Aberdeen, and seamen from Liverpool, who all jostled each another in the courtyard. Most of the Bay men were Scots by birth or extraction, and all of them gentlemen by company standards, though of a relatively unpolished variety.

Fort Vancouver quickly became the headquarters and nerve center of HBC business. From there, runners were dispatched with news and orders to Colville with word that fifty horses were needed at Fort Nez Perce to outfit the Snake brigade; to chief trader Samuel Black at Fort Nez Perce that an American trader had slipped up the river to The Dalles and that Black was to reduce company prices temporarily; to John Work, leading a trapping party to northern California, where he was to meet Michel

Laframboise and his men at the Umpqua; to William Connolly at Bear's Lake in northern Caledonia that leather was needed at Fort Colville.

Doctor John proved to be an able administrator and was eminently successful in carrying out Simpson's plans for agricultural development and diversified trade. He was confident when dealing with the natives, whom he understood. However, subject to orders that he considered inappropriate to local conditions or with a crisis in his personal life, he panicked, suffered from a nervous stomach and exploded in violent temper.

George Simpson, who had been schooled in ruthless business practices in the sugar and slave trade of the West Indies, through his personal friendship with Andrew Wedderburn, deputy governor and chief executive of the London HBC committee, had the sympathetic ear of the entire body, who in turn were urged by crown officials to 'do their duty' to the government.

'Men of the country', or French Canadians, replaced imported Orkney men from the rugged islands of northern Scotland to paddle the canoes. The governor, expressing his prejudice – for he believed that God himself had assigned men to their respective positions – reported that as crewmen Canadians were 'active and indefatigable' and therefore preferable to Orkneymen, who were 'of slow and inanimate habits'. The latter were cheaper, however.

Canadians, in Simpson's opinion – and you could not cross his views without being charged with treason – were a 'volatile, inconsiderate race of people, but active, capable of undergoing great hardships and easily managed by those who are accustomed to dealing with them'. Orkneymen did not possess the same physical strength and spirits necessary on trying occasions, were 'obstinate and extreme' and 'guarded'. Irish and Scots also were to be avoided, being naturally quarrelsome, independent, and inclined to form leagues and cabals. The fact that Doctor John shared not a single one of these traits did not appear to influence Simpson in the slightest.

At Fort Vancouver, five primary languages were spoken – English, French, Tshinuk, Cree, and Hawaiian. Cree was the language spoken in the families of the many officers and men who married native women at posts east of the Rockies. Hawaiian was in use among the hundreds of natives of the Sandwich Islands who were employed as laborers. Besides these were Chehalish, Walla Walla, Kalapuya, Nisqually, Clackamas, Multnomah, Skillute, Cathlamet, Cascades, Chinook proper, Clatsop Chinookans, Molalla, Klickitat, Yakama, Wasco, Wishram, Umatilla, and Tillamook, who all spoke the omnipresent Chinook Jargon that everyone understood.

The word 'Indians' was never used by these people. They did not regard themselves as such and did not respond to the term. It was a grab-bag label used to denote an enormously complex and divergent range of cultures, primarily by the same people who hoped to exterminate them and claim their land. These were not Indians as understood in the history books. They were something else.

Such was the polyglot nature of the fort, from the very beginning.

2.2

One of the Americans who George Simpson hated most was Jedediah Smith, surely one of the most peculiar trappers who ever lived.

Jedediah had a dry sense of humor and did not use profanity – ever – at a time when mountain men were known for their foul language. Members of his family were staunch Christians, although assertions that he carried a Bible with him in the wilderness were newspaper nonsense. The only thing ever verified by witnesses was that he said a prayer at the burial of a massacre victim. He did not drink alcohol or bed native women, which was part of his strict moral code.

However, Smith owned two slaves, which went completely against his Methodist upbringing, and his behavior was anything but honorable when dealing with natives. He wrote of the Maidud natives in Mexico that they were 'the lowest intermediate link between man and brute creation'. During a trek across the Great Basin, he described the natives as 'children of nature, unintelligent beings that form a connecting link between the animal and intellectual creation'.

Jedediah was a spectacularly handsome man, a New Yorker by birth and a New Englander by heritage, an explorer whose mappings led to the twenty-mile-wide South Pass as the dominant point of crossing the Continental Divide on the Oregon Trail. While trying to obtain fresh horses and get a notion of where on Earth he was, he was attacked by a grizzly bear that ripped open his side and took his head into its mouth. The men who found him held up his scalp and ear, which had been completely ripped off. Smith calmly and soberly convinced a friend to sew them back on with a needle and thread. After recuperating, he wore his hair long to cover the scar from his eyebrow to his ear. The American press went nuts over the incident. Handsome white guy ripped apart by bear recovers. It was enough to make headlines across the country, perfectly fitting the stereotype of American rugged individualism.

The foundation of his reputation, however, was due to a skirmish in Oregon in which twelve people were killed. Smith was the first to start the fight and the last to give it up. The newspapers on the East Coast loved the story.

In Oregon country 300 miles south of the Columbia in 1828, Smith's party of nineteen came across some natives, and when a chief among them reportedly buried an ax in the sand while trying to steal it, Smith's party treated them harshly. One native was forced off his horse at gunpoint, and Smith had another tied up until the ax was produced. On July 14, 1828, while Smith and two others scouted a trail north from the Umpqua River, the natives attacked his camp and killed fifteen men.

On August 8, 1828, Arthur Black arrived at the gates of Fort Vancouver badly wounded and almost naked, having traveled 300 miles to safety in a panic. He thought he was the only survivor of the attack and did not know of the fate of Smith and the two others who had gone scouting. A successful attack on whites without a response was a sign of weakness on the part of the HBC as the only law in the land, and Doctor John began organizing a search party to go after the survivors. However, before they left Smith and the two others arrived at the fort.

Doctor John sent Alexander McLeod south to rescue any men who might have survived, and when they reached the camp they found eleven decomposing bodies. All fifteen of the unaccounted-for men had been killed. McLeod subsequently recovered 700 beaver skins and thirty-nine horses that belonged to the dead trappers.

The full story of the massacre at the Umpqua came out slowly. It turned out that on July 11 the company reached the estuary of the Umpqua River and in the afternoon a few natives wandered into camp. They were Kalawatsets, but they weren't a tribe, they were a group of Coos, Kuitsh, and Siuslaw. One of them took an ax, and Jedediah seized the offender, bound him, and ordered him held until restitution was made. The man was a chief. To lay hands on him was to offend the dignity of the entire tribe. The ax was returned, and the hostage was released.

The next morning it rained and the Americans drove their animals four miles through the mire and halted at the Umpqua River. The Kalawatsets visited them again, fifty or more this time, to trade beaver skins, fresh berries, and the information that fifteen or twenty miles farther on there was easy traveling across the coast range to the Willamette River. Jedediah rose early the following morning and set off with two of his men to find the trail, leaving orders with Harrison Rogers that no natives were to be allowed in the camp. That order wasn't followed. The Kalawatsets crowded in accompanied by women, who were brought as a symbol of peaceable intent.

When McLeod arrived, the Kalawatsets were respectful, but they said the Americans told them that their land belonged to the United States and that Americans would soon come in huge numbers and drive out the British, who did not hunger after their land. McLeod managed to get out of a witness that the massacre happened after Rogers had tried to rape a native girl.

The lesson in this for Doctor John was that the natives usually told the truth, while HBC officers and men told the truth most of the time, and Americans seldom, if ever, got the facts straight, preferring to tell the story in a manner that best suited a newspaper report full of melodrama and cliches. In the end, the murders went unpunished since the HBC figured that Jedediah's party had brought it on themselves.

Jedediah, however, was a welcome guest at Fort Vancouver and stayed there for some time. Doctor John didn't see him as an opponent who had to be exterminated but as an educated, civilized explorer who had a wide range of stories to tell. When Smith returned to Fort Vancouver with McLeod on December 14, 1828, Simpson was there visiting and diplomatically offered to buy what beaver skins had been recovered, along with the horses. Smith had no real choice. Altogether, he received $2369.60, which was a lot of money at the time. In return, he agreed that his fur company would confine its operations to east of the Continental Divide. Things were so cozy for him that Smith remained at Fort Vancouver until spring, when he and Arthur Black went east to meet their partners.

I was too young at the time to be allowed to see much of him, but I recall that he was a strapping, virile man who even the natives respected. The life he lived was the stuff of legend even in his own time. A few years after visiting Fort Vancouver, Jedediah was killed by Comanches at a watering hole near the Cimarron River while he was en route to Santa Fe, and I cried when I heard the news. He must have known the risk, but he took it anyway, as he did with all things in his life. I won't ever forget him even though I never got the chance to speak to him directly.

2.3

Fort Vancouver sat at an envious intersection of tribal trade that ran east-west along the Columbia River and north-south along the Willamette Valley and Puget lowland. By 1824, the year before Fort Vancouver was built, the sea otter population on the Pacific Coast was virtually gone and the supply of furs from the Columbia River estuary and adjacent coast was dropping off precipitously. The land-based fur trade was eclipsing ship-based pelts, and Hudson's Bay Company leaders looked to the interior as a source of furs. The shift from a sea-based to a land-based fur trade also brought increased interaction between white trappers and tribes.

There was good reason the Chinooks and Cowlitz maintained their trade monopolies with Fort Vancouver. The wealth and status of their chiefs was elevated by the HBC policy of working through tribal leaders. Comcomly, Casseno, and Scanewa became dominant in a way that would have been difficult to envision only a short time before.

In short order, Fort Vancouver and the lower Columbia tribes became dependent on each other.

So strong was their bond that when the Wascos attempted to attack the fort because the HBC proposed moving a trading post out of their territory, they were stopped when Casseno intervened. His word was enough to halt the attack. When a fire threatened to burn down Fort Vancouver, natives nearby jumped in to save the fort since saving it was in the interests of the Chinook and Cowlitz tribes. When two young natives plotted to assassinate Doctor John, one of the youths took fright and confessed after he was told that his fellow natives would not put up with it. Doctor John escaped injury, but the incident was instructive. Not all people loved him, and some were even willing to murder him.

On October 25, 1828, there was a squeal of bagpipes and a loud knocking at Fort Vancouver's front gate. It was totally out of keeping with the bucolic nature of the place. It was Saturday, so there was no school that day, and we children were free to entertain ourselves as we saw fit, so we scurried out to see what was happening.

George Simpson had arrived on an inspection tour. By that time, things were going to his head and he had acquired vice-regal tastes. At every post the entire company was formed into a procession. Simpson strutted in the front done up in a beaver plug and Micawber collar, a piper leading the way before him, a gigantic Scot whose kilts aroused serious interest among native maidens who wanted to see what was under it. The whole thing was less a wilderness tour than a royal procession.

However, Simpson brought with him two vital pieces of information. First, he'd found that the canyons of the Fraser River were not navigable after all, which came as no surprise to anyone else. On his westward journey, he traveled up the Peace River into New Caledonia, then struck south down the Fraser. The river's wild white water soon convinced him that my great-great-uncle Simon Fraser was right after all, the river was not navigable. Second, the diplomats of Great Britain and the United States had not been able to agree on a boundary between the two countries and the joint occupancy agreement was extended indefinitely. However, either country could terminate the agreement by giving the other a year's notice.

Doctor John had been very successful at implementing Simpson's agricultural plan. He installed two sawmills, one beside a small stream five miles east of the fort and the other twenty-five miles up the Willamette River at a point where a waterfall crashed in clouds of mist over a ledge of dark basalt, a spot that Simpson visited and agreed had enough lumber to supply the entire British navy for years to come. He therefore ordered Doctor John to build a ship, *The Vancouver*, a sixty-ton schooner. It was built but was barely seaworthy and was used on the lower Columbia where there were few waves to knock it over. A better job was done on the thirty-ton sloop *Broughton*, launched the same year, 1826, but a serious lack of skilled labor, scarcity of iron, and lack of properly seasoned timber forced abandonment of any further shipbuilding efforts, much to Doctor John's relief.

HBC now had two ships, and this meant that the original fort on the bluff would have to be abandoned in favor of a new complex closer to the river and its docks. Doctor John hated ships. His experiences with sea captains had been uniformly negative. They were prone to drunkenness when in port and believed that they were in command and no one else could usurp their authority.

Simpson, however, loved ships. He wanted to be like the Americans and sail up and down the coast picking up furs brought from inland and resupplying the forts by water. His dream was to build a depot on the Fraser River at Fort Langley and circumvent Fort Vancouver entirely. When that didn't work, he envisioned HBC headquarters on Vancouver Island. Anywhere the Americans could not infringe on British authority, which meant on his own authority. Doctor John took charge of the vessels and made them strictly auxiliary to the new posts, including Fort Simpson in 1831, Fort McLoughlin in 1833, and Stikine in 1840.

After four years on the bluff overlooking the Columbia, Fort Vancouver then was moved to the floodplain above the high-water mark. Under Doctor John's direction, the post soon contained more than thirty buildings, including warehouses, carpenter shops, smithies, a bakery, store, schoolhouse, chapel, living quarters, and Doctor John's house in the middle, where the men dined every day at noon to discuss the day's business. Outside Fort Vancouver, natives camped according to their own design.

In addition to not relying on ships, Doctor John didn't want the natives armed. 'If they are not animal hunters, guns are of little or no use to them in procuring food', he wrote. Virtually all guns came by ship, and so did alcohol. His naval people tended to be drunks who were careless with the natives. Drunkenness disgusted Doctor John. He recognized the dangers in what became a wholesale ship-to-shore trafficking in liquor and women.

The effort required to relocate the fur-trading center from Fort George and construct an entirely new site at Vancouver belies the importance of the move. Simpson had to do the bidding of the London committee, and for him to succeed on the Columbia a rare personality and character was required. Simpson didn't have it. He couldn't go off the grid and call the shots himself. Even so, he was always on the lookout for ways to embarrass Doctor John, if not to imperil him entirely. It was a strange relationship.

Simpson from the start wanted more posts built along the northern coast and more ships to retrieve furs, the same as the Americans had done for years without establishing a single fort. Simpson even suggested that his shirttail cousin Aemilius Simpson consider a few of the Americans who had been in service on Yankee coasters because they knew the native dialects and also because he believed Americans worked harder and demanded less than his own people. However, his plan didn't go anywhere. There was too much prejudice among the gentlemen in the Hudson's Bay Company to allow such a thing.

Aemilius Simpson took his flagship, the *Cadboro* – which was not much longer than the seagoing canoes of the north – to the mouth of the Fraser River in the summer of 1827 to cover James McMillan while he built Fort Langley, the planned entrance to the interior that would have circumvented Fort Vancouver had the Fraser River proved to be navigable. It was there that George Simpson met his first real Americans. They appeared to him to be wholly insignificant people, 'jumped-up tradesmen,' he called them, common trappers parading around with empty military titles, little men who formed thinly financed groups to conduct a marginal trade and be a nuisance to their betters. Those were his prejudices. In fact, he came face-to-face with a foe who would outmaneuver him and win the war no matter how many minor battles he won.

At the same time, half a dozen Yankee peddlers were beating their way up the coast from California to Alaska, paying prices for furs that Doctor John considered ruinous but still turning a tidy profit. Veteran American trader Captain John Dominis brought the brig *Owyhee* into the Columbia, followed shortly by a well-laden supply ship, the *Convoy*. In a confrontation designed to warn HBC to stay out of the maritime fur trade, Dominis began offering the Chinooks sensational prices for their furs. Hoping to drive Dominis out of the river, Doctor John reactivated Fort George, cut prices below those offered by the Americans, and sent traders out to the native camps in an effort to have the furs come to them.

The first of HBC's supply ships, the *William and Ann*, smashed up on the Columbia bar in 1829 with the loss of its entire cargo and all twenty-six crew members. A second ship, the *Ganymede*, arrived from England, and using fresh goods from the ship Doctor John spent seventeen months countering every single move made by the *Owyhee* and the *Convoy*. At the same time, he took care of one of Dominis' sick mates, provided the American captain with potatoes and lumber, and thwarted native plans for an attack on the ships. In July 1830, the Yankees finally left, having collected at ruinous prices 2,900 skins and fifty-three barrels of salted salmon.

HBC was paying five times as much for furs as they'd calculated. 'I think it is so important to make our opponents pay high for everything they get', Doctor John wrote. He sent out land parties to buy up all the available furs in the area, and after the *Owhyee* sailed in 1830, the *May Dacre* was the only American ship to enter the river for the next ten years, and its visit was connected to a private venture to construct an American trading post.

2.4

Beginning in the 1770s, smallpox skipped up the coast from Mexico and killed thousands of natives even before the first explorers arrived. In 1830, the 'cold sick,' or malaria, began working its way up the river, and the natives believed that Dominis and the Boston ship had intentionally released the sickness on them. The one who was left to deal with the mayhem was Doctor John.

The year 1829 was a disease year, the start of something momentous. Disease had broken out the previous year among natives living near where the *Owyhee* was stationed off Deer Island on the lower river. Americans called it 'fever and ague', the British called it 'intermittent disease', and the natives called it the 'cold sick'. It reached Vancouver in summer 1830, coming on with devastating force and prostrating even Peter Ogden. A large man, he was reduced from 300 pounds to a bony shadow of his former self by the epidemic.

At one time, more than seventy people at the fort were hospitalized – exclusive of women and children, who were not counted – and operations almost came to a standstill. When the resident surgeon made the sick list, Doctor John added medical duties to his other chores, dosing patients with powdered dogwood bark when the fort's supply of cinchona ran out.

The native tribes were nearly wiped out. They clustered in wretched bands around the fort pleading to be allowed to remain where there would be someone to bury them after they died. With reluctance, Doctor John ordered them to be driven away, believing they were a threat to the health of his own people. They went into the bush to die wholesale, and entire villages were left devoid of life, save except for the dogs that scavenged among the rotting corpses.

While the natives died, most of the whites survived. The victims at Fort Vancouver were given quinine, then dogwood bark boiled in water, which was the standard treatment for malaria. The patients generally recovered. By contrast, the native treatment of a sweat lodge proved lethal. 'The remedy generally did its intended work', said John Dunn. 'It cured the disease but killed the patient.'

Comcomly died in 1830 along with forty of his children. The Chinook tribes were reduced from twenty-five strong tribes to eight weak ones. A population of Chinooks and Kalapuyas estimated at 15,545 was cut down to 1,932. Casseno lost 2,000 members of his tribe and his immediate family, consisting of ten wives, four children, and eighteen slaves, which were reduced to one wife, one child, and two slaves.

'Within the houses, all were sick', visitor John Townsend reported. 'Not one escaped the contagion. Upward of a hundred individuals – men, women, and children – were writhing in agony on the floors of their houses with no one to render them assistance. Some were in a dying struggle and clenching with the convulsive gasp of death while their disease-worn companions shrieked and howled in the last sharp agony'.

Comcomly, despite a sumptuous burial in a canoe, was not allowed to rest in peace. Doctor Meredith Gardner, the Hudson's Bay Company physician, cut off Comcomly's head one night in 1835 and sent it to England for study. Gardner, following a native curse, died in the Sandwich Islands not long after stealing the skull.

Change is inevitable, but change of this kind was calamitous. Everything on the lower Columbia had to be rearranged. Meanwhile, one of the most dangerous of native tribes, the Cayuse on the upper river near The Dalles, avoided the whole thing by taking to the hills and waiting it out. The Cayuse had a tendency to think of themselves as superior to other natives in much the same way that the Americans thought of themselves as superior. Escaping near annihilation only reinforced that belief. As chance would have it, the Cayuse were squarely in the path of immigration that would take place in the coming years. Cold, taciturn, and high-tempered, they fought less for territory than for booty and glory.

All in all, the stage was set for disaster.

2.5

The northwest corner of the United States was the last part of the country to be settled. So little was known of this terra incognita that some thought Salt Lake was an arm of the sea. Others thought a great river called the Buenaventura flowed from the valley of Salt Lake through the western mountains, emptying into the Pacific at San Francisco Bay. If such a river existed, it would have been a great avenue for shipping furs. It didn't exist, so attention turned to the Columbia.

Modern history began in 1828 when William Sublette brought the first wagons over the plains to the Rockies. He coaxed ten 1,800-pound freight wagons from St. Louis to the fur-trapper rendezvous at Wind River, Wyoming, over a route that presaged the history of one of the most spectacular migrations the world has ever seen.

Jedediah Smith rode with those wagons back to St. Louis, where he wrote a letter to the secretary of war, John H. Eaton, noting the exact opposite of what George Simpson had spelled out in his talks with Smith. This would give rise to the Oregon fever that carried Americans by the thousand over South Pass, along the Snake River, and down the Columbia.

In 1817 – coincidentally the same year that I was born – a fellow named Hall Jackson Kelley had a vision. In it, God came floating down out of the clouds in a blaze of glory and anointed Kelley with a sword, declaring him a special agent of providence. God charged him specifically with carrying Christianity to the heathen of the Pacific Northwest. Immediately, Kelley set up a howl for the colonization of Oregon, bombarding Congress with petitions and the press with letters and pamphlets, careening from one town to the other like a drunken evangelist, revealing 'the truth' to whoever would listen. In 1831 Kelley produced 'A General Circular to All Persons of Good Character Who Wish to Emigrate to the Oregon Territory,' in which he contended that Oregon was the most healthful spot on the face of the planet. He proposed that an enormous emigrant party be formed to march across the continent and settle on lands purchased from the natives by a joint-stock company. Kelley himself would guide the emigrants.

He didn't go to Oregon in 1832 as planned, but another member of the colonization society did, Nathaniel Jarvis Wyeth of Cambridge, Massachusetts. Wyeth was production manager for Frederick Tudor, who pioneered the shipping of ice to the tropics. What Wyeth proposed was to revive John

Jacob Astor's plan of twenty years earlier and establish a post on the Pacific, supply it with ships out of Boston, and send those same ships back loaded with with furs and salmon. The plan looked logical on paper. Wyeth had no idea of the Bay's monopoly on the Columbia and no way of knowing the odds against his success. He hoped to establish himself so strongly that, once the Convention of Equal and Open Occupancy lapsed, he would have a monopoly on American trade in the area. Meanwhile, Kelley took off on an adventure of his own to reach Oregon – led by God, of course. Kelley and Wyeth wouldn't reconnect for two years.

Wyeth recruited twenty members for his stock company and reached St. Louis in April 1832. That city, which had already seen its share of remarkable and supremely odd characters, beheld the stunning sight of twenty-one men dressed exactly alike in striped shirts, wool pants, and rawhide boots carrying bayoneted rifles and small bugles to communicate in case they got lost, which with this bunch was extremely likely. They hauled with them three boat-wagons beautifully constructed so they could sail across rivers and waterways en route. The mountain men marveled at the boats – then kindly pointed out that the heat of the plains would bake open the seams in a flash and the amphibious wagons were nothing but prairie fodder. Wyeth wisely jettisoned the contraptions.

At Independence, Missouri, Bill Sublette looked on in awe, took a liking to the brash American, and informed him that he was being crazy. Sublette took the bunch in tow, getting his brother, Milton, to guide them the rest of the way. Bill Sublette recognized Wyeth as a potential rival to the Hudson's Bay Company, but not by the remotest stretch of the imagination a threat, even though he would have liked him to pose a commercial presence.

While all this was happening, the company began to unravel. Two men deserted twelve days out. Many of the rest were completely naive and unaware of the realities of frontier life. Like the Americans who George Simpson ridiculed, they allowed their horses to wander off on their own and stuffed things like pots and pickets under their pack saddles so they could escape quickly with provisions. About all this did was render the poor animals sore-backed and useless.

The rendezvous was at Pierre's Hole west of the Tetons, and the Wyeth group reached it on July 8 with only eleven men. Two of the defectors were members of Wyeth's own family who had gotten a notion of the idiotic sight they presented, including his brother Jacob, the company surgeon, and a nephew, John. They went back home and immediately began to write about the absurdity of the expedition.

On July 17, Wyeth and company set off once more, traveling for safety under the tutelage of Milton Sublette, and on the evening of October 14 reached

Fort Walla Walla, only a hundred miles from their destination.

Doctor John heard all about the gyrations of Hall Jackson Kelley even from a distance of 3,000 miles. When Nathaniel Wyeth pulled into Fort Vancouver, Doctor John smiled at the audaciousness of it, if nothing else, and like Bill Sublette took an instant liking to the American, who always preferred to travel at full gallop on his horse. It was the sort of aggressiveness the chief factor could appreciate, and besides, Nathaniel Wyeth was a nice guy.

At Fort Vancouver, the worst news awaited Wyeth. The brig he had hired to bring supplies and goods for trading had grounded on a reef in the South Pacific and was lost. Only the friendship and respect of Doctor John remained. Without that, the naive Wyeth could not have survived on his own for long dealing with the natives, who were some of the shrewdest businessmen in the world. Doctor John came to the quick conclusion that his guest was not colonial-minded and would never mount a serious economic threat. It was better to let Wyeth be a lesson to the world. Besides, under the joint occupancy agreement, Wyeth had a perfect right to be there. In the end, Doctor John missed one salient point. Thirty years after Lewis and Clark had crossed the country, the path had been so well marked that even novices could follow it to the Oregon country. This was the beginning of the wave of 1830, which commenced with the bleak obliteration of most of the natives.

One of the people who came to the Columbia was James M. Bates. He was born in Washington, D.C., went to sea in 1827, and during the next year found his way to the Pacific Ocean. His ship put into Gray's Harbor to refit in 1829, and the crew went in boats up the Chehalis River, coasted southward, and wintered at Scappoose, where they raised vegetables.

In the spring, they went north to Sitka, and returning entered the straits of Juan de Fuca, took a load of horses to the Sandwich Islands, and sold them. Bates proceeded on another ship to China, then returned home via the Cape of Good Hope. In 1837, still a sailor, Bates came to Oregon in the *Don Quixote* and joined the missionaries as a blacksmith. In 1847, he married Margaret Caldwell and settled there.

2.6

Interracial marriages gave Hudson's Bay Company a remarkable degree of control over the personal lives of employees and the women the men married. HBC officers sought to place tight restrictions on these 'business marriages', as they called them. Employee relationships with spouses prohibited infidelity and attempted to regulate spousal abuse, fearing a threat to company security and profitability. The company was prone to severely punish anyone whose amorous relationships put the fur trade at risk.

Many of these wives were Cree or Canadian Metis, having arrived on the Columbia from other places within the Bay's range of operations. Children of interracial marriages were considered especially desirable marriage partners for the ambitious young officers of the day. Marguerite McLoughlin and Amelia Douglas, the wives of Doctor John and his assistant, James Douglas, both were part Ojibwe. Marguerite and Amelia set the standard for native wives at the fort, being the public face of Bay charitable efforts within Kanaka Village, where rank-and-file workers lived just outside the fort gates.

These marriages were not without troubles. Anxiety over potential abandonment plagued many of the women. Desertions were commonplace in light of the mobility of fur traders and the expiration of their contracts. Men who had been reassigned to other Bay posts often simply left their wives and children behind. George Simpson and chief trader Dugald McTavish both abandoned their half-native wives for British women in 1830, events that received much attention in the forts and inspired many similar actions among lower-order officers. Also, the absence of church-sanctioned marriages allowed Bay men to disentangle themselves and return home at the end of their service with few legal ties to bind them.

The position of the Bay on abandonments was mixed, but Doctor John himself was rigorous in his attempts to dissuade employees from jettisoning their wives. HBC usually allowed men to bring their families with them when they transferred to a new post, and pressured employees to provide for their families if they did not bring them along. The Bay did not subsidize moving families, but Doctor John facilitated moving between posts or arranged for abandoned women to receive support. The fort grudgingly supplied widowed or abandoned women with rations, but only at Doctor John's orders. He went so far as to have individuals flogged for refusing to care for their children. Marriages were sometimes arranged – in many cases by Doctor John himself –

between women who were abandoned or widowed and single men working for the company.

Virtually all the men, including Iroquois, Hawaiian, and Metis, objected to head-flattening. The men were universally firm. They did not want their offspring disfigured by having their heads flattened in the Chinook custom, and the vast majority of the native wives were Chinook. Chinook women who wanted to avoid conferring the cultural stigma of a round head on their children either had an abortion or set the infant out to die.

As a place where single young women met single young men, accounts of Fort Vancouver describe it as a place of great sexual tension. That wasn't true, having been there to witness this myself. The allegation was used by missionaries as evidence of licentiousness, a charge that fort officers often had to counter in their official correspondence.

Stopping these liaisons was virtually impossible, however. The fort's officers were resigned to romantic relationships. Efforts made to restrict contact between employees and native women by superior officers went very badly. Murders of Bay traders have been traced to efforts to contain amorous liaisons between fort employees and local women. It was small wonder that Bay officers kept such relationships at arm's length and hesitated to intervene.

A good example was Dr. Forbes Barclay, who was born in the Shetland Islands on Christmas Day 1812 with a cleft palate. His father was a prominent physician who lectured on anatomy at Edinburgh and authored a book on the movement of muscles. Barclay studied medicine in Edinburgh and spent several summers as a surgeon with exploring expeditions to the Arctic. One of these voyages ended in shipwreck, but Barclay was among the survivors rescued by the Eskimos.

He was granted his medical diploma by the Royal College of Surgeons on July 5, 1838, and appointed surgeon to the Hudson's Bay Company in 1839.

Traveling around Cape Horn by ship, he arrived at Fort Vancouver in 1840, where he was immediately put in charge of the hospital, which he described as an old shed outside the stockade. He also doctored the settlers and natives in the region.

A chief factor, Pierre Pambrun, died as the result of a fall from a horse in May 1841, and soon after his wife Catherine Pambrun moved her children to Fort Vancouver, where she did needlework to support them.

Barclay fell in love with their daughter, Maria Pambrun, when he was thirty years old and she was sixteen. Her acquaintanceship with Barclay began with the family's arrival at the depot since they were housed in the bachelors' quarters and the library was housed there also, which Barclay oversaw.

The couple moved to Oregon City after Doctor John retired in 1846, having decided to cast their lot with the Americans. Barclay's practice ranged across the Cascades as he traveled on horseback and by a canoe navigated by a native guide. The romance was fairly typical of the frontier liaisons that permeated Fort Vancouver.

2.7

At this time, the vacant half of the chief factor's house came to be filled. William Connolly, who was in charge of New Caledonia, found a large mulatto, James Douglas, to be a 'fine steady active fellow, good clerk and trader, well adapted for a new country' and chose him to assist him in opening an overland route for pack horses from Fort Alexandria on the upper Fraser River to Fort Okanagan at the junction of the Okanogan and Columbia rivers. The brigade traveled 1,000 miles from Fort Stuart to Fort Vancouver. It was a celebrated event when it arrived, and it was one of the only times I can remember that Doctor John could be seen drinking a glass of wine in public.

James Douglas had decided on retiring from the fur trade after having gotten fed up with the isolation, lack of companionship, lack of good books, the hostility of the natives, and the danger of starvation. Then he met Amelia Connolly, William Connolly's daughter, and they got married 'in the custom of the country', which is to say without a priest or minister, there not being one around for a thousand miles.

Connolly left Douglas in charge of Fort St. James while he took the furs to Fort Vancouver in 1828, and a tumult with the natives ensued. Douglas could be furiously violent when aroused, and once he'd determined that a native had killed a Bay trader, he took umbrage, stalked into the nearby village, pulled out a gun, and shot the man in the head in full view of witnesses. Lots of stories were concocted to veil this incident and shield the Hudson's Bay Company, but that's what happened.

Members of the Carrier tribe took an immediate dislike to Douglas as a result. It wasn't a question of whether the native was guilty or not, it was simply not Douglas' place to take such matters into his own hands. The relatives of the dead man were the ones who had the right to extract retribution, not him, and by doing so he violated a prime native prerogative. 'Douglas' life is much exposed among these Carriers', Connolly reported to George Simpson in February 1829. 'He would readily face a hundred of them, but he does not much like the idea of being assassinated'.

Connolly's recommendation was that Douglas be transferred to Fort Vancouver, and on January 30, 1830, Douglas left Stuart Lake to become an accountant under Doctor John.

I won't forget Douglas' arrival. He did not preen and strut as he entered the fort as George Simpson had done, but with his sword at his side he stood humbly and obediently, yet almost monarchical in his bearing. The natives called him 'black Douglas' because he was descended from the dark-skinned people of South America. Moreover, he was black because of his outlook. Unlike Doctor John, Douglas was a die-hard British loyalist who believed to the depths of his being that he was the king's subject and wanted to set an example for the world to follow.

Douglas arrived without his wife, Amelia, who was heavily pregnant with their first child and stayed behind at Fort Stuart. From the get-go, he was stalwart and forthright, and employees and natives both looked up to him. Doctor John took an immediate liking to Douglas, so much so that he invited him to occupy the other half of his house. It was an interesting pairing. Both were uppity, in the words of Casseno, the native leader in those parts, meaning that their word was law and none other needed to be observed or obeyed. In fact, both had virulent tempers and tried hard to keep their emotions in check. Doctor John had been involved in a similar incident, and was transferred to the Columbia as a result.

An exact man to the minutest detail, Douglas pleased Doctor John. His accounting was impeccable and made the fort look good, which pleased Simpson. The fact that the books weren't always accurate didn't appear to bother either Doctor John or Douglas. They were in agreement about how things looked on paper.

The fact that Douglas was almost slavishly loyal to the crown was not lost on George Simpson. He noted the fact for future reference, especially when it contrasted with the suspected loyalty of Doctor John, who no matter how he tried to conceal the fact always acted like an American – somebody more like Jedediah Smith or Nathaniel Wyeth than a British citizen.

Douglas had one unfortunate tendency. As the officer responsible for Columbia headquarters when Doctor John was gone, he sought to elevate moral standards. In particular, he was disturbed by the presence of slavery. 'With the natives, I have hitherto endeavored to discourage the practice by the exertion of moral influence alone', he informed the London committee. 'Against our own people, I took a more active part and denounced slavery as a state contrary to law; tendering to all unfortunate persons held as slaves by British subjects the fullest protection in the enjoyment of their natural rights'.

Later, when a chaplain who had been sent from England, the Rev. Herbert Beaver, proved to be a religious fanatic, Douglas declared, 'A clergyman in this country must quit the closet and live a life of beneficent activity devoted to the support of principles rather than of forms; he must shun discord, avoid uncharitable feelings, temper zeal with discretion, and illustrate precept by example'.

What he really meant was that those standards of behavior were his own ideals.

Unfortunately, Amelia Douglas arrived empty-handed. Their child hadn't lived long and was buried at Fort Stuart. With sadness, she delved into her duties at Fort Vancouver with vigor in order to forget. My mother, who had been alone for so long, now not only had a helper to assist in her hostess duties but by incredible good fortune had an accomplice who was part Ojibwe and spoke the language. The two gabbled in such profusion that even I, who knew the language well, was hard-pressed to understand what they were saying.

2.8

In the summer of 1830, I was thirteen years old and had lived on the lower Columbia for nearly half my life. I was for the most part sequestered. My mother, father, brother, and I lived in half the house. The Douglas family lived in the other half. In the middle was the public mess where the important men and guests of the day took their meals, sitting according to rank. At a separate table on the side, native chiefs and their legions ate in accordance with their own social customs. Mother acted as hostess, serving the men. This was the age at which I began to be admitted as her assistant.

David at that time was nine years old, a curious, restive boy who favored native boys as playmates. He often skipped off with them off into the wild, and being part Ojibwe himself was treated like any other native child. He hunted and fished and played at being a warrior and counting coups, which meant that he touched the enemy and lived to tell about it. One of his favorite times was at the evening campfire when he was called upon to talk about his day's adventures in detail and reap praise if his exploits were daring enough. His time in the fort by comparison was heavily circumscribed. He was forbidden from doing any of this and admonished accordingly.

David had not been formally educated or sent off to school at a young age as his older brothers had been. Instead, he was tutored inside the walls of the fort by whoever was at hand at the time. David would not get his first formal schooling until Doctor John enlisted the aid of John Ball. The agenda did not call for me to be educated, since I was a girl, but I was nearly as headstrong as my father and complained vociferously when David was allowed to run amok outside the gates of the fort but I was not. As a compromise I received informal tutoring.

Ball was Oregon's first schoolteacher. He was a strict constructionist who celebrated only two holidays, the Fourth of July and Thanksgiving. To him, Christmas was a pagan holiday. Ball picked up his education from reading the Bible, hymn books, Webster's spelling book, Morse's geography, and Adams' arithmetic. Stuffy as he was, especially for an American, he was a good teacher and we learned a lot under his tutelage. My education, of course, was not official, but Ball took this in stride and although he did not approve of it accepted the fact that Vancouver was not his puritanical home state but a horse of a different color, a hybrid if you will.

Ball was credited with establishing the first American farm at Champoeg, but became disenchanted with the primitive life and returned to New York in 1833, then moved to Michigan, where he spent the remainder of his life.

Doctor John himself was a great history buff. He read incessantly and could quote Herodotus at length. In addition, he was a great fan of Napoleon, not so much for his battles but for his maneuvering and tactics. Ideas that now underpin the modern world – meritocracy, equality before the law, property rights, religious toleration, modern secular education, sound finances – were championed and codified by Napoleon. It was how Napoleon accomplished these things that intrigued Doctor John. Napoleon wasn't original; he simply took the centuries-old precepts of Machiavelli to heart and followed them.

Machiavelli wrote that princes who rose to power through their own skill and resources rather than luck had a hard time reaching the top unless they effectively crushed their opponents and earned respect. They could afford to make compromises with allies only when they were strong and self-sufficient. Moreover, it was impossible for a prince to satisfy everybody. Inevitably, he will disappoint some of his followers. Therefore, a prince must have the means to force supporters to support him even when they have second thoughts. Otherwise he will lose his power.

Yet, you cannot call it virtue to kill your fellow citizens, betray your friends, and to be without faith, without mercy, or without religion. Such techniques enable you to acquire an empire but not any glory. It is glory for which we are most remembered. Savage cruelty, inhumanity, and infinite crimes do not permit a prince to be praised. Machiavelli – and by application Napoleon – advised that a prince should carefully calculate all the wicked deeds he needs to do in order to secure power, then execute them in a single stroke. In this way, his subjects eventually forget the cruel deeds. Princes who fail to do this and hesitate in their ruthlessness have to keep a knife by their side as they can never trust their subjects.

These were the lessons Doctor John passed on to me as the one nearest at hand and very possibly the only one who was interested. He would constantly relate these views to my mother, but her experience was different. She knew perfectly well that men tend to live in a bubble of their own making while women do all the hard work. The way Doctor John took this to heart and applied it was key. He put the two together and ruled over his fiefdom with an iron hand. At the same time, he tolerated transgressions if they were for the good of the whole. It was an anomaly, to be sure, but it was well thought out.

David was not amenable to this kind of learning. He was vastly more interested in finding out what a river sturgeon ate and how to bring one of those leviathans in on a line without getting pulled off your perch. Yet, like our father, he was a quick study and did what was required of him.

This era was pivotal for all of us. The old powers could no longer rule because the old order was no longer intact. It had been decimated by disease. As many as nine in ten natives who lived along the lower Columbia and its tributaries perished from malaria, smallpox, measles, and other diseases. It was hideous to watch, yet there was nothing we could do about it. We hoped and prayed that the natives would recover, but they did not. Day in and day out, word came to us that an old friend or someone we respected had died. Their spirits were free, but that didn't do the living much good.

For our part, we had to live with the fact that they died and we did not. It made no sense even to the good doctor, who aided all supplicants and dealt harshly only with con artists and chronic ne'er-do-wells and manipulators. He maintained his empire in good order for the benefit of all, but especially for the benefit of his family. Of this I was a prime recipient. It would be impossible for me to relate how this affected me. It was both terrifying and exhilarating. We were forming our own characters, establishing our own futures, and no one was there to do it for us.

Many notable people of the time visited Fort Vancouver, such as naturalists John Townsend, David Douglas, and Thomas Nuttall. Before summer 1830, I did not have the ability or opportunity to meet many of them, having been kept apart. But I knew who they were, and my father told me about them.

From that summer on, everything was different. Not only had the times changed but so had the philosophical situation.

For one, I had come into my own as a woman, having reached marriageable age – though I had no intention of doing so. I was allowed to mingle with these personalities for the first time and even to talk to them on occasion. I was deputy hostess under my mother's tutelage and got to attend at least one of the daily meals at the public mess. As I sat on the sidelines unobtrusively waiting to whisk away a plate or serve a dish, I witnessed many of the conversations that went on. It was an education in itself. Likely, there was no other place in the entire world that could have matched it. My descriptions from here on are less observation and more participation. I was becoming one of them.

2.9

During the winter of 1828-29, George Simpson ordered Doctor John to buy land at Willamette Falls for a possible industrial site. Doctor John was told to secure title to the property on behalf of the company. He did as ordered but held the property in his own name, not in the Hudson's Bay Company's, since this was likely to become American territory. He erected some small buildings, blasted a millrace on Abernathy Island, and planted potatoes on the east bank. Later, he had a warehouse built as a summer HBC post and timbers hauled to the island for a sawmill.

Doctor John maintained that he wanted the place for a retirement residence even if it was expected to be in American territory. Not even the British had any realistic hopes that the area south of the Columbia would end up in British hands. This issue would come to haunt Doctor John in his later years.

When Nathaniel Wyeth arrived on the Columbia in 1832, Doctor John knew he came as a competing trader but welcomed him cordially, granted his group credit since they were ragged and destitute, and offered Wyeth a seat at his table. Wyeth's journal on October 29, 1832, read: 'Arrived at the fort of Vancouver. Here I was received with the utmost kindness and hospitality by Doctor McLoughlin, the acting governor of the place. Our people were supplied with food and shelter. I find Doctor McLoughlin a fine old gentleman, truly philanthropic in his ideas. The gentlemen of this company do much credit to their country by their education, deportment, and talents. The company seem disposed to render me all the assistance they can'.

Wyeth believed he could grow wealthy in Oregon as a rival in the fur industry, developing farms for growing crops, especially tobacco, and establishing a salmon industry to rival New England's cod market. His expedition had proceeded along the Oregon Trail up the Platte River, through the Black Hills, across the Grand Tetons, and swung north of Great Salt Lake in Snake country to Fort Nez Perce, where Pierre Pambrun of the Hudson's Bay Company arranged transportation down the Columbia to Fort Vancouver. Captain Benjamin Louis Eulalie de Bonneville, a Paris-born army officer on extended furlough, was traveling in the West in the guise of a trapper when his expedition took the first wagons over South Pass, yielding the most accurate maps of the Rockies and the Great Basin of their time. In a report to the War Department in July 1833, Bonneville described the Willamette Valley as 'one of the most beautiful, fertile, and extensive valleys in the world, wheat, corn, and tobacco country'.

Wyeth sold the patent for his horse-drawn ice-cutter to his company for $2,500 in order to buy supplies for his expedition. He counted on trapping his way west, and therefore invested the money in arms, supplies, and equipment, including 480 five-pound beaver traps with double springs, jaws without teeth, and two-swivel chains six feet long.

However, the country beyond the Green River had been denuded of beaver, the result of George Simpson's policies, and Wyeth did not catch his first beaver until late in August. Several days after Wyeth arrived at Fort Vancouver, he got that news that his supply ship had sank in the South Pacific, and he wrote that 'my men came forward and unanimously desired to be released from their engagement with a view of returning home as soon as possible. ... I am now afloat on the great sea of life without stay or support but in good hands – i.e., myself and providence'.

Two of his companions settled in the Willamette Valley, becoming the first Americans to do so.

3.1

George Simpson saw little danger from settler incursions. He believed that settlers could not come by way of the Columbia River since the only route was across the bitter Snake River country, which had nearly defeated the undoubtable Peter Ogden in the winter of 1824-25. Few could survive such a trip, and those few who did would be sure to arrive destitute and unable to establish a farm. Simpson wanted Fort Vancouver to shut its gates to the settlers and send them back on the trail to California.

Doctor John did not agree with Simpson that the idea of settlers making their way over the mountains was untenable. He not only didn't agree that it was impossible, he told Jeremiah Smith – who ought to know, being an explorer – that not only was it likely but perfectly logical. Now he had the chance to discuss it over meals with Nathaniel Wyeth, an amiable man. Wyeth became more sophisticated in his arguments and presentations as time went on. Yet, Doctor John held the upper hand. He knew that without extensive resources Wyeth's plan would fail because it would be necessary to offer cut-rate deals and bear the cost in order to establish a market. Only the Bay had the resources to do that.

What Doctor John knew and others didn't was how shrewd and in control the Chinooks were. You underestimated them at your own peril. Now that disease had decimated their numbers, Doctor John agreed they were at a disadvantage, but only a temporary one, for he felt their numbers would rise again. These arguments served only to increase Nathaniel Wyeth's determination. Doctor John wished him well but remained skeptical about his outlook and warned Wyeth not to try his sales tactics in Oregon country. The situation there was too unpredictable, and if he succeeded he would have to face Doctor John, for whom he clearly was no match. Doctor John acted the gentleman but remained deeply suspicious of Wyeth. 'Though it may be as he states, still I would not be surprised to find that his views are in connection with a plan I see in a Boston paper of 1831 to colonize the Willamette', he wrote.

Wyeth left to return to the East with Francis Ermatinger, who was headed to HBC's Flathead Post. Wyeth and his men then moved on with Benjamin Bonneville to the 1833 rendezvous at Horse Creek. Before leaving, Wyeth negotiated with Milton Sublette and the Rocky Mountain Fur Company to furnish them with $3,000 worth of supplies for the next rendezvous. He reached Liberty, Missouri, in late September and from there went to Boston. The expedition wasn't a commercial success, but Wyeth brought with him a collection of plants previously unknown to botany.

Wyeth reached Cambridge on November 6, 1833, and immediately began to plan a second expedition to the Columbia. By year's end, he had raised $20,000 for a startup he called the Columbia River Fishing and Trading Company. By February 1834, he was ready to leave and in a letter to his wife, Elizabeth, who was left alone again with their three children, he offered instructions on trimming the trees around their Cambridge house along with an apology for his lack of warmth: 'I have many letters to write and am unused to writing to ladies anyway'. How she felt about all this was not recorded.

The Wyeth caravan of seventy men and 200 horses and mules departed on April 28, 1834. Accompanying the expedition was Methodist minister the Rev. Jason Lee, and during the early weeks of May Lee encountered his first natives, the ones he'd come to save for God. They were Kaws, a branch of the Osage tribe, and bore no resemblance to the natives cited in the storybooks. The adults were half-naked, the children entirely naked, they hadn't washed in months, and wherever they went they were surrounded by a pack of mongrel dogs as thick as flies. They were thievish, importunate, and slowly starving to death.

'They appear in the most rude and uncivilized state of any human beings I have ever seen', commented Cyrus Shepard, a mission schoolteacher.

Even after Lee learned that they were starving and dying, he refused to share a single ounce of the food he'd brought along to establish a mission. 'Lest', he wrote in his journal, 'we should not have enough until we reach the buffalo'.

Wyeth had taken to calling himself Captain Wyeth, and no one objected. Any man who had found his way over the mountains and back was qualified to call himself whatever he wanted to in the minds of the trappers. He continued west with my half-brother Thomas McKay and established Fort Hall in southeastern Idaho. McKay guided them to Fort Nez Perce.

McKay kept his ears open the whole time. Wyeth's party headed to the rendezvous on Hams Fork with 13,000 pounds of goods and reached it on June 19, 1834. William Sublette found out about the contract between Wyeth and the Rocky Mountain Fur Company and forced the company to forfeit the contract. Wyeth arrived at Fort Vancouver on September 14, 1834, and was hospitably received by Doctor John and the other forty-seven gentlemen at the fort. The brig *May Dacre* with Wyeth's supplies on it was at that time in the Columbia. However, damage from a lightning strike at sea had forced the *May Dacre* into a Chilean port for repairs, causing the brig to miss the entire spring salmon season and costing Wyeth over a year's worth of trade.

Wyeth immediately established a post on Wapato Island downriver from Fort Vancouver at a point where disease had wiped out a native village. Within a week, he had erected a forge and charcoal house there, laid out a farm, and gave orders for the post to be called Fort William. Wyeth had stocks of raw alcohol and the makings of a still brought round Cape Horn on the *May Dacre*. It was the beginning of a commercial war between it and HBC, but at least it was a warfare on honorable terms.

Wyeth chose Wapato Island for good reason. Upon seeing the deserted villages caused by the disease epidemics and finding no one around to object, he figured that God was speaking to him, although in not so illustrious a manner as God had spoken to Hall Jackson Kelley.

'So you see', Wyeth concluded, 'as the righteous people of New England say, providence had made room for me'.

Methodist missionaries also arrived on the *May Dacre,* but by that time the pestilence had burned itself out and only a thousand or so scattered Kalapuya survivors remained in the entire Willamette Valley. These natives were culturally dazed, demoralized, and dirt poor. Wyeth arrived as the fur trade was going into decline, and the Methodists arrived when there were no more natives left to convert.

On the *May Dacre* also came two naturalists, Thomas Nuttall, curator of Harvard Botanical Gardens, a respected authority on botany and ornithology, and John Kirk Townsend, a practicing physician and self-taught ornithologist who would go on to make a name for himself as one of the best-read authors on the Oregon Trail.

Doctor John wrote in his notes on Wyeth: 'In justice to Mr. Wyeth, I have great pleasure to be able to state that as a rival in trade I found him open, manly, frank, and fair. And, in short, in all his contracts, a perfect gentleman and an honest man, doing all he could to support morality and encouraging industry in the settlement'.

Wyeth, persistent to the end, renewed his proposal for cooperation, and Doctor John finally agreed, much to the displeasure of his superiors. He was fearful that Wyeth, with his tenacity and fortitude, would establish a supply line of his own if he refused, and he was also confident that Wyeth's enterprise would fail.

After Wyeth got to Fort Vancouver, who should arrive a month later but his old cohort Hall Jackson Kelley. He had taken two years to get from Boston to Oregon, a period during which Wyeth had come and gone twice. Ewing Young and his party brought Kelley to Fort Vancouver the month after Wyeth arrived, wrangling a herd of 200 mules and horses to trade. Before they got there, Doctor John received a letter from the Spanish governor of Alta California, Don Jose Figueroa, notifying him that the horses had been stolen. These marauders, Don Jose suggested using the standard epithet for Americans, should be apprehended and punished, or at the least deprived of their booty. Young said he had stolen no horses but admitted that others in the group had.

Kelley arrived in the company of these men. None of that altered his expectations, which were to dine at the high table and be put to bed with fresh linen. Instead, Doctor John assigned him to a dirty hut that stank of old fish outside the fort's palisade. Doctor John offered food and free medical care, but Kelley was not received in the bachelors hall where visiting dignitaries were customarily housed. Kelley therefore convinced himself that he was the victim of corporate persecution, since even the Americans avoided him. Young and his friends would continue to be banned from dealings with any Hudson's Bay Company employees current or retired. Young, who was already rich from trading horses, laid out an enormous claim on the west side of the Willamette River, built a cabin, put his animals out to graze, employed his companions – excepting Kelley, who he blamed as the reason for his problems – and sat down to sulk.

Kelley's story is worth noting. He taught school in Boston and promoted the moral reform of 'fallen women' as the founder of the Penitent Female Refuge Society. His textbook 'The American Instructor' sold well and continued to support him even after he left Boston schools.

On his way west, he was robbed by his own companions and by the Mexican government as well. Eventually, he came to La Paz at the tip of Baja California and from there worked his way north. From San Diego, he made it by ship to Monterey, where he ran into Ewing Young. In August 1834, a column filed out of San Jose driving thirty-nine horses north, and Kelley, Young, and the five men in Young's command were joined by nine hard cases who 'volunteered' to come along with their horses and were accepted because it was clear that they would have killed Young, Kelley, and everybody else if they hadn't been invited along. The better part of good sense was to let them come to Fort Vancouver.

On the way, the newcomers murdered, raped, and plundered with delight all the natives they came across, and Young and his men could do nothing to stop them. In the Sacramento Valle, they all were stricken with malaria, with Kelley the sickest of them all. The group debated leaving him behind and going on without him when the party met the Bay's returning California brigade commanded by Michel LaFramboise, which held enough firepower that it easily could have overcome even the rapacious cowboys. LaFramboise took Kelley in charge, dosed him with Peruvian bark and venison broth, and on October 27 helped him through the gates of Fort Vancouver.

The Rev. Jason Lee, the preacher who had come over on the *May Dacre*, regarded Kelley's schemes as a threat to his own ambition for a Methodist-dominated republic in the Willamette Valley and visited him only surreptitiously. Wyeth called on his old friend Kelley only one time.

Kelley was all in all not a very likable fellow. He wore a white slouched hat, blanket capote, leather pants with a red stripe down the seam – rather outre even for Vancouver – and besides, he was labeled a horse thief.

After being housed, fed, and ignored all winter, Kelley went home hating Doctor John as a 'prosecuting monster' and continued his crusade for an all-American Oregon, originated a scheme to send a colony to Oregon to build a city on the east side of the Willamette River at its junction with the Columbia, and to build another city on the north side of the Columbia River opposite Tongue Point. He didn't realize that the land was a swamp and nothing could be built on it.

Lee for his part was not exactly sympathetic to the plight of non-Christians in his midst. After arriving at Fort Vancouver, he stared in wonder at the neat buildings – storehouses, gristmills, threshing mills, sawmills and the thirty or more log huts of company servants. The dazzlingly white clapboard chief factor's house dominated the quadrangle, which had views of snowcapped Mount Hood and was surrounded by hundreds of acres of wheat, barley, peas, corn, melons, pumpkins, squash, peach, and apple orchards, and arbors of grapes. By that time, Fort Vancouver's herd of California cattle had grown to nearly 700 head.

Lee's only comment: 'The Indians are a scattered, periled, and deserted race ... it does seem that unless the God of heaven undertake their cause they must perish off the face of the Earth and their name be blotted out from under heaven.'

In 1832, when Wyeth's first expedition collapsed and left several men stranded on the Columbia, Doctor John hired John Ball to teach six young boys, including his son David. I, Marie Eloisa McLoughlin, slipped into the group. Ball didn't last long but was followed by another of Wyeth's men, Solomon Smith, and then by a trained teacher, Cyrus Shepard, who arrived with Jason Lee in Wyeth's second expedition.

3.2

At the time, waifs roamed the village due to abandonments. When an employee left the Oregon country, he often simply jettisoned his family. The forsaken wife sometimes walked away from her children and returned to her own tribe. Or, a wife would run away with a native lover and leave her husband to take care of the kids. Doctor John gathered up eighteen of these derelict children and used school as a means of keeping them out of trouble so they didn't prey on natives and Bay workers. Doctor John was particularly anxious that all the youngsters learn English. He hung a leather badge as a dunce cap around the neck of any student who lapsed into French.

There were other examples of auspicious lives at Fort Vancouver.

Howard C. Ashworth was an English adventurer who was discovered in the Rocky Mountains scrounging food from American trappers during Nathaniel Wyeth's second expedition. He arrived with the group at Fort Vancouver on November 5, 1834. The expedition included two missionaries who were given the luxury of a room inside the fort, and Ashworth secretly moved in with them. An incredulous Doctor John, who saw through this charade, escorted him out but allowed him to have biscuits, potatoes, and salmon until Ashworth joined the HBC brig *Eagle* ten days later as a passenger bound for the Hawaiian Islands.

Webley J. Hauxhurst ran away to sea as a young man. He deserted ship when he reached California and spent three years in Monterey as a furniture maker and carpenter before coming to Oregon with Ewing Young in 1834. With funds from Doctor John, he built the first grist mill in Oregon in 1834. He became the first white convert of the Methodist Mission, abandoned his 'intemperate ways' and became a leader in the church. Hauxhurst was subsequently elected to the board of the Oregon Institute in 1843 and served on the first board of Willamette University. During the California gold rush, he had a successful business making pack saddles.

Clerk Francis Ermatinger caught his native wife in an affair with a man from her own tribe. He sliced off the fellow's ears with a hunting knife and turned his wife out of doors. He sought schooling for his young son Lawrence, then withdrew him and sent him east to be educated by his brother. Although the children at Fort Vancouver were fed well, they were poorly supervised and developed dirty habits and scandalous morals, he contended.

3.3

In 1829, George Simpson expressed a desire to go to England to seek medical attention. Although he wasn't ill, he contended that constant traveling was taking its toll on his health. There was another, more pressing reason: he wanted to find a marriage partner.

Simpson's attitude toward natives and people of color extended to women as well. Before marrying, he fathered a huge number of illegitimate children – as many as seventy by one count. Simpson made provisions for most of these children, but they were kept at a distance.

In 1817, he produced a daughter by a half-Cree washerwoman named Betsy Sinclair. She was soon passed on to an accountant who Simpson had promoted. He fathered two sons, George Stewart in 1827 and John Mackenzie in 1829, with Margaret Taylor. Soon after the birth of John Mackenzie, Simpson left Margaret to get married. He shocked his peers by neglecting to even notify her of his marriage, much less make arrangements for the future of his two sons.

Simpson treated his mixed-blood wives as sex objects, and his manner of disposing of them manifested no feeling whatsoever. He called them his 'bits of brown'. Since he fancied himself as royalty, he felt he could do as he pleased.

Sailing from New York, he was in London by October 21, 1829, and during the winter found a 'suitable' partner. That turned out to be his cousin, the daughter of Geddes Mackenzie Simpson. Her name was Frances. She was eighteen, and he was in his forties.

Simpson suddenly began taking a strong line opposing marriages between fur traders and native women, then left it up to Doctor John to enforce the rules. It goes without saying that Doctor John, his stomach tied up in knots, ignored these orders, establishing instead a thriving village outside the fort walls where workers built their own dwellings according to company plans and maintained their families, which usually involved native wives.

The couple married on February 24, 1830, and after a brief honeymoon sailed from Liverpool to North America. Simpson embarked on a working honeymoon, dragging his bride halfway around the world. Although she was violently seasick on the ocean voyage, her health improved enough after their arrival in Montreal for her to enjoy the canoe trip from Lachine to York Factory in Manitoba. She was awed by the magnificence of the scenery, admired the strength and skill of the voyageurs, two of whom were entrusted to carry her bodily over portages, and was amused by the gallant attempts of the company's officers to welcome her. Eventually they landed in Red River, where George Simpson ordered the building of Lower Fort Garry with the intention that it would become their official residence.

As one HBC officer said, Frances was a 'pious creature who resigns herself patiently under all circumstances, which will contribute to the honor of her gallant knight'.

Frances Simpson's arrival had serious repercussions, however. Most HBC officers had native wives, but after the British marriage of George Simpson, who had cast aside a native wife and family, racial prejudice increased by leaps and bounds. Simpson determined that native women, regardless of the rank of their HBC husbands, should be excluded from polite society, especially in the Red River settlement where the Simpsons took up their winter residence. Frances fully supported her husband's decision to exclude them, believing that her own heritage outranked the base births of such women.

The transition from London proved to be too much for Frances. She had no friends, and from the time of her arrival in 1830 suffered from poor health. Simpson was a devoted husband, but the difference in their ages and his autocratic ways produced an insurmountable gulf between them. Both returned to

England in 1833, where it was decided that Frances should remain and not return to North America with Simpson in 1834 but instead would stay in Scotland, where she remained for the next five years and gave birth to several children as a result of his visits.

By that time, George Simpson had become a man of substance in both Canadian and British circles. His superiors in London listened to his advice with respect, and he often wrote the very instructions that they supposedly sent to him. There was never any question that the ultimate authority rested with the London committee, but so long as he made money he was allowed to do pretty much as he pleased.

After the return of Frances Simpson to London in 1833, she received the best medical attention available yet remained a semi-invalid for the rest of her life. Her husband had the habit of treating her like a child, and five subsequent pregnancies continued to weaken her. Frances Simpson was suitable breeding stock, but otherwise she was on her own.

She wasn't the only one who had a string of bad luck in the fur trade. William Brown, after sailing to Hudson's Bay, made his way overland to Fort Vancouver. There, in the early 1830s, he caught 'intermittent fever', or malaria, which kept recurring. On May 11, 1834, while unloading cows at Nisqually, he was gored in the testicles.

Brown took a wife at Fort Langley but when he tried to leave the service he was held back at Fort

Vancouver because his wife had died and left a child under twelve months old to be cared for. When he refused to return to Langley and look after the child, Doctor John hit him three times with a rod until he agreed to care for the infant. He returned to Langley, where a nurse was provided, and boarded at company expense for the next year.

By August 1838, he was told that he had to leave the service with his child, so he made his way to York Factory and returned home to England in 1839. The child eventually returned with Brown when he came back, and they settled in the Willamette Valley.

3.4

Each Sunday, as Hudson's Bay Company rules required, Doctor John assembled the fort's commissioned gentlemen, workers, womenfolk, and visiting natives in the main hall and read to them the Church of England service. Then he added Roman Catholic readings in French, ostensibly for the voyageurs, but also for himself.

Workdays were long – a rising bell at five a.m., labor for an hour or two before breakfast, then another long stint before midday dinner. Afternoon was broken by tea, and work continued until nine p.m. Following a light supper, the clerks retired to their quarters, where some held impromptu concerts or read. Doctor John's preference was for history.

Food for the gentlemen was prepared in a separate kitchen connected to the dining room by a covered passageway. One of the fort's clerks was responsible for drawing up the menus and deciding how the dishes were prepared. Cooking was done by French Canadians and Hawaiians. A specialty was black pudding, a concoction of blood, fat, and spiced pork stuffed into a gut. It looked awful, but it tasted good. Wine was served on formal occasions. Doctor John sipped only enough to put his guests at ease – a sure indication that everyone was watching him closely to avoid breaches of etiquette. Seniority was strictly observed. The lower one's rank, the farther from the head of the table he sat.

Unless addressed with a direct question, junior clerks at the far end seldom said a thing.

For their dawn-to-dusk work, laborers were paid on average £17 a year. They were given huts tolive in and were provided with a weekly ration of eight pounds of potatoes and eight pounds of salted salmon. Otherwise, the men had to buy items such as bread and tea at the company store. Purchases were charged against each worker's account, for clerks and other officers thirty-three percent more than the invoice cost in London; workers and seamen were charged fifty percent; and people not connected with the company were charged double, a matter of grievance to American settlers when they found out about it.

All the officers tried to convey the impression of gentlemen. They wore white shirts and broadcloth suits to dinner. When faced with a long horseback ride, they switched to leather pants to save wear and tear on their trousers, but they always wore a tall beaver hat and protected it from the rain with an oilcloth cover. Neither Doctor John nor James Douglas, both burdened with fiery hot tempers, used profane or vulgar language, and they imposed that standard on all their subordinates.

Doctor John and Douglas held diametrically opposing views on how pleas for assistance should be handled. A stern British loyalist, Douglas thought newcomers should be given just enough to help them survive so they would quickly move on to California. Doctor John argued in favor of offering them credit for as much seed, livestock, and equipment as the fort could spare. His reasoning was that if he refused requests the migrants would seize what they needed and burn down the log fort out of vindictiveness. Accordingly, he extended newcomers unsecured credit eventually totaling £6,606, a figure that shocked George Simpson when he found out about it. As matters developed, much of that debt was never repaid.

Many of the settlers brought with them searing anti-British prejudices, and also anti-Catholic prejudices, the result of Protestant teachings. The settlers looked on the Hudson's Bay Company as a heartless foreign corporation dominated by economic and religious tyrants.

Women were sequestered from many of the formal affairs of the fort. They were not allowed in the dining hall, and the wives of the gentlemen were generally kept away from visitors.

The wives of officers held special standing in the fort, overseeing the organization of social events and helping host visiting women. Many of the officers' wives were Cree or Metis, arriving from other places within the Bay's range of operations, and employees often married into local tribes. Marguerite McLoughlin and Amelia Douglas were both part Ojibwe and set the standard for native wives at the fort, being long-term partners to their husbands, gracious hosts to visitors, and the public face of charitable efforts in Kanaka Village.

Hawaiians served in a variety of capacities, all under the general classification of servants. In addition to being laborers, they were classified as mill workers, sailors on both the river boats and ocean ships, gardeners, soldiers, and cooks. All employees were expected to perform any task required, including guard duty, farm labor, maintenance work, anything associated with paddling or portaging canoes, and cleaning, drying, sorting, and baling furs.

This policy applied to all fort employees including physicians, who were required to serve as clerks when not busy with medical work. In practice, the Hawaiians worked as shepherds, sawyers, cooks, coopers, and woodcutters or stokers on steamships. They were sometimes paid a small bonus for special assignments or for particularly loyal service to the officers.

Servants were provided with weekly food rations that varied depending on the supply. One example was '4 Quarts Peas, ½ lb Tallow, 9 lbs Salmon, and 3 lbs bread or Potatoes'. On occasion, fresh meat was made available when hunters brought in extra game. These rations were extended to servants, but not to their families. A few exceptions were made for widows with children, but since a servant's ration was seldom enough to feed himself much less his family, women were obliged to earn money to buy extra food. Wives worked as farm laborers and salmon processors and in the manufacture of candles, portage straps, and other items sold in the company store. Things such as tea, coffee, molasses, liquor, and condiments were considered luxuries and could be bought only at the company store.

Some of the Hawaiians married native women in the village, as did the Canadian Metis. Many had their children baptized even though they were the offspring of unsanctified marriages. Under HBC strictures, women and children were to be furnished with 'regular and useful occupation as is suited to their age and capacities, and best calculated to suppress viciousness and promote virtuous habits'. The HBC employee was instructed to address and encourage his wife and children to use his language, be it French or English, and to 'devote part of his leisure hours to teach the children their catechism'.

With the growth of the school-age population, formal schooling was provided at Fort Vancouver for children starting with the arrival of a teacher in late 1832. A succession of teachers, including a clerk, a voyageur, and a clerk's wife, taught classes first in the dining hall and later in a school room in the stockade. At various times, classes included a day school for children and an evening school for boys and young men. At maximum attendance, the school had about 60 sixty scholars, one-third of them girls.

Many of the workers sought to ameliorate conditions by using slaves, who not only performed household chores but also hunted and fished for additional food. It was the native wives of employees who introduced the captives to their new homes. In 1833, London abolished slavery and HBC could hardly condone lawbreaking. However, efforts to free household slaves met with resistance and the workers' wives often sent them to live with relatives in nearby villages where their lot often was worse than before. The slaves themselves many times preferred the security of servitude to the uncertainty of freedom.

A trained teacher, Cyrus Shepard, arrived in 1834 with the missionaries Jason and Daniel Lee, and was available to teach school. Most of the HBC engages, however, saw little point in educating their offspring and instead put them to work at an early age.

George Traill Allan was typical of many personnel. He was a well-known clerk with the Hudson's Bay Company and in later years a storekeeper at Oregon City. He was an affable, intelligent man of slight build, five feet tall, and weighed one hundred pounds.

He was nicknamed Twahalasky, or coon, by the natives because they thought his face looked like a raccoon. He retired and became a commission merchant until he settled in Cathlamet for good.

3.5

Early on, establishing a herd of pigs at the fort proved to be a difficult proposition. In 1836, Doctor John wrote to the company's directors in London saying, 'There is a weed on our plains, which poisons a great number of our pigs, but it will get extirpated'. The Hawaiian Naukane, known by the name of John Coxe after a shipmate who died when Fort Astoria was founded, solved this problem. As a child in 1779, Naukane had witnessed the death of Captain Cook in Hawaii. In 1811, he was appointed by King Kamehameha I as a royal observer to accompany twelve Hawaiians employed by the American Fur Company in Astoria. He returned to Hawaii in 1814, and in 1823 accompanied King Kamehameha II to London on an ill-fated journey to visit King George IV.

Kamehameha and other high-ranking members of the court traveled to England, arriving there in May 1824, and for nearly a month toured London. By June, many members including the king had contracted measles. On July 8, the queen consort Kamamalu died. Days later, Kamehameha II died. The bodies were returned to Hawaii for burial but Naukane and others in the traveling party who did not come down with measles were forever after regarded with suspicion. Naukane therefore returned to his life in the fur trade and his identity as John Coxe in order to escape scrutiny, becoming a swineherd at Fort Vancouver. Coxe was joined by fellow Hawaiians Orohuay and Towai, both pigherds, who grazed the pigs on the plain between the fort and the Columbia River, an area that came to be known as Coxe's Plain.

Amable Arquoitte entered service as an HBC middleman in 1823. He went to California in 1849 for three months during the gold rush, then settled on a claim and became a naturalized citizen. He was permanently blinded while helping blast a millrace around Willamette Falls at Oregon City. He was the father of nine children with his Chinook wife. His marriage year was officially 1839, when he was married by arriving priests.

In March 1835, Jackson Hall Kelley sailed for the Sandwich Islands on a Bay vessel with money provided by Doctor John. He found his way back to New England, taking eighteen months to do so, and never returned to Oregon. He remained fixed in his conviction that he was the sole architect of Oregon's colonization and would write pamphlets defaming the preachers Jason and Daniel Lee, entrepreneur Nathaniel Wyeth, and Doctor John. He constantly asked Congress to grant him a suitable reward for his efforts, without success. In his eighties, having slipped into madness, he came to believe that the street urchins where he lived were agents of the Bay who had been sent to spy on him.

William Johnson was an Englishman who went to sea as young man. He joined the Hudson's Bay Company as a tracker, settled at Champoeg in 1835, and took up farming. In 1842, he left his farm and moved to Portland, where he began distilling a concoction known as Blue Ruin that gained him local fame.

In the spring of 1835, eight men and the trail wife of one of them left San Francisco to ride overland to Oregon. When they reached the south bank of the Rogue River, they were attacked by the tribal cousins of two young warriors who had been wantonly murdered the year earlier before by the Young-Kelley party. Two of the whites were killed outright and two more were so badly injured they could not travel and had to be abandoned and left on their own. The remainder escaped, although one of them was hideously wounded.

That was William J. Bailey, a young British physician. An ax sliced through his lips just below the nose, split his jaw, and was driven deep into his neck, narrowly missing the carotid artery. In this condition he managed to stumble 300 miles to the Willamette Valley, his shattered face bound up in a filthy handkerchief, arriving at the Mission House with his bone and flesh half-healed into a lumpy distortion. From that point on, surgery could no longer do him any good.

In a day when young ladies were expected to be silent and submissive, Margaret Jewett Smith was neither. She attended Wilbraham Academy against the wishes of her father – who believed that education for women was an abomination – and prevailed upon the Methodist mission board to appoint her as a teacher in Oregon. On the voyage out, she looked after the Rev. David Leslie's children.

Things did not go well between her and the reverend. Long before the party reached Oregon, the two were no longer on speaking terms.

One Sunday Margaret Smith invited some natives to church services. When they marched in, the Rev. Leslie asked them to sit outside on the front steps where they would be 'ventilated by the breezes'. Affronted, they went away and never returned. Smith became a principal organizer of the Oregon Female Benevolent Society, which was formed to teach native women how to sew and by charitable example to improve their lot.

William Holden Willson served as cooper on a whaler, knocking together the barrels in which oil was stored, and set off in pursuit of Margaret Smith. He won her trust but omitted to tell her that he was already betrothed to a young lady in Connecticut named Chloe Clark. Margaret somehow learned of

Chloe's existence and the fact that Willson had dispatched a letter of proposal to her. Margaret considered herself betrothed, but she stubbornly refused to agree to marriage until she had proof that William's invitation truly had been withdrawn.

At the outset of winter, it was decided that the two of them could share a single cabin, but Margaret replied firmly that there would be no question of matrimony so long as doubts remained. Willson replied that immediate marriage would be excused should a young lady from the east subsequently appear. Margaret told him hotly that their engagement was at an end. Willson ran from the house shrieking that he would get revenge upon her and sought out Brother Beers, the sternest of the Methodist saints, to announce that he was in trouble, saying that he had sent for Chloe Clark to be his bride but had since sinned grievously with Sister Smith. Willson was urged to repeat his confession in front of the congregation, and he did so with loud lamentations, tearful in his repentance. Margaret proved recalcitrant, protesting her innocence all the while.

The Rev. David Leslie was forced to issue an ultimatum: she also must acknowledge her transgression, for the brethren would accept no less. Having no recourse, she signed the confession. She was forced to admit wantonness, which in a woman was beyond the forgiveness of the mission family. Not long afterward, she married Doctor William J.

Bailey of the scarred and misshapen face. Shortly thereafter, he was licensed to preach. The heralded Chloe Clark subsequently showed up, and William Holden Willson was duly married.

Such were the travails of the Methodist Mission.

Rev. David Leslie arrived in September 1837 accompanied by his wife, Mary A. Kinney, and their three children. Then his wife died in 1841, leaving him with six children. While she was ill, their house burned to the ground along with all their possessions. After her death, his oldest daughter, her husband, and her younger sister drowned at Oregon City when they were swept over the falls. Another child died in the Sandwich Islands while she was visiting with her father. He then married Adelia Judson and died in Salem.

3.6

In December 1835, the ship *Neriede* dropped anchor off Vancouver. This was when the Methodist minister the Rev. Daniel Lee disembarked, nephew of the Rev. Jason Lee, along with the Rev. Herbert Beaver of the Church of England, London's chaplain-designate to Fort Vancouver, along with his wife, Jane. Ironically, only a bit later a freight canoe manned by company natives slipped up to the fort's landing and five white strangers got out. They included Marcus Whitman and his wife, Narcissa; the Rev. Henry Harmon Spalding and his wife, Eliza; and William Henry Gray, a carpenter-mechanic. These Americans had not only crossed the mountains successfully, pioneering the Oregon Trail, but had brought their women with them, something that had been deemed impossible before that. These newcomers were not Methodists but Presbyterians sent by the American Board of Commissioners for Foreign Missions.

Narcissa Whitman was markedly pregnant at the time and the ladies stayed on as guests. Doctor John urged them to remain at the fort even as London was criticizing him for helping the Methodists and for his hospitality to Americans in general. His reply to the London committee was hotly indignant.

Doctor John did what he could to confine the missionaries to the Willamette Valley south of theColumbia. The more Americans who settled on the north side of the river the stronger the American claim to that area. He convinced Jason Lee to establish a mission in the Willamette Valley instead of going north into Flathead or Nez Perce country, as Lee originally planned. But the Whitmans could not be dissuaded from settling among the Cayuse at Waiilatpu near Walla Walla. Doctor John pleaded with them, explaining that the Cayuse were hostile and unpredictable and that he thought the Spaldings would have much better success converting the Nez Perce to Christianity. However, he also argued that it would be far safer for them if the Whitmans stayed in the Willamette Valley. They were Presbyterians, however, and all those people were Methodists, a distinction that only the warring parties could appreciate.

Narcissa charmed the people at Fort Vancouver. My mother became her favorite companion, and they took long rides together, Marguerite riding astride her horse like the native women did, while the proper lady from the east rode clinging to her sidesaddle. Narcissa marveled at the cosmopolitan life at the fort. Each course at the table was served on a fresh plate, there was wine – although the missionaries declined to drink any of it on pious principle – and the gentlemen frequently toasted each other.

Narcissa tutored me. Nearly every evening, she sang with the children of the French Canadian trappers and their wives. Narcissa tried hard to make friends with the natives, leading the children in singing, teaching them to read, and participating in religious services, but they frightened her.

'The Old Chief Umtippe has been a savage creature in his day', she wrote in her diary. 'His heart is still the same, full of all manner of hypocrisy, deceit and guile. He is a mortal beggar, as all Indians are'.

The fact that she called them Indians was a telling remark since they themselves never referred to each as other as such. It was a pejorative Western label driven by a misunderstanding that began when Christopher Columbus mistakenly thought he'd discovered the nation of India instead of the island of Hispaniola.

Doctor John gave James Douglas the job of taking the fort's accounts to York Factory, and in 1835 he attended the council meeting at the Red River Settlement. There, on June 3, he was given his commission as chief trader. During Doctor John's absence in England in 1838-39, Douglas had charge of Fort Vancouver, the coastal posts, the trapping expeditions, and the shipping. In November 1839, he was promoted to chief factor, a promotion that gave him financial security. A most frugal man, by spring 1850 he had accumulated savings of nearly £5,000.

In 1838, Jason Lee proposed a massive expansion of the mission field, and new stations were established near the mouth of the Columbia, at the lower end of Puget Sound, at Willamette Falls, and at The Dalles. Their stated purpose was to serve the needs and save the souls of the heathen inhabiting those areas. It just happened that every single site at which a mission station was erected was a place of enormous commercial potential, indicating that the Methodists had far more in mind than the salvation of souls.

An attempt was made to find families in Europe that would settle at Cowlitz and Nisqually on the north side of the river and farm on half-shares on behalf of the Hudson's Bay Company, thereby giving England grounds to claim the north side of the Columbia as its own territory. Since prospective settlers could not obtain ownership of the land, none of them signed on and HBC had to content itself with recruiting twenty-three families from among the Metis of Red River near Winnipeg, Canada. That emigration disturbed the Americans south of the Columbia, and so did the appearance of two Catholic priests sent out to minister to the French Canadians of Oregon.

The Rev. Francis N. Blanchet was one of the earliest Catholic missionaries to the Northwest, arriving at Fort Vancouver in 1838 from Canada along with the Rev. Modeste Demers. The pair traveled widely throughout Oregon and Washington establishing churches, and Blanchet worked at Fort Vancouver and in the country south of the Columbia. He became archbishop of Oregon and died in Portland.

The Protestants believed the Catholics meant to bind those people more firmly to Fort Vancouverand thereby give the British better claim to the north. That did not prove to be the case, as the priests only spread goodwill among the natives, who were more inclined to adopt Catholic rites than they were to accept the more harsh tenets of Protestantism.

Even the aid that Doctor John extended to the fifty-one men, women, and children who arrived by ship in 1840 to join the Methodist mission had scant effect on American audiences, who continued to maintain their conspiracy beliefs. As it was, the Cowlitz and Nisqually settlement failed when every one of the families took off for the American side of the river and settled permanently in the Willamette Valley, where they could gain ownership to their land.

3.7

Nathaniel Wyeth's second expedition in 1834 brought the first Methodist missionaries, including the Rev. Jason Lee, along with several lay teachers, arriving on September 17, 1834, by way of the *May Dacre*. Boats and men were furnished by Doctor John to the missionaries so they could to explore the country and select a proper place for their mission.

Doctor John wrote: 'I observed to them that it was too dangerous for them to establish a mission north of the Columbia, that to do good to the Indians they must establish themselves where they could collect them around them; teach them first to cultivate the ground and live more comfortably than they do by hunting; and as they do this, teach them religion; that the Willamette afforded them a fine field and that they ought to go there and they would get the same assistance as the settlers. They followed my advice and went to the Willamette'.

Jason Lee accordingly selected a spot on French Prairie about ten miles north of Salem. Doctor John placed at his disposal a boat and crew to transport the mission's goods from the *May Dacre*. He loaned them seven oxen, one bull, and seven cows with calves. Moving goods and cattle to the mission required several days, and he also provided a manned boat for the missionaries. Without these, the mission would never have come into existence.

Doctor John knew perfectly well by that time there were very few natives left to convert in that area and that the Methodists were intent on establishing ties with the United States. He was powerless to prevent them from taking up residence under the occupation agreement, so he steered them in that direction, since it was going to occur no matter what he did.

As early as 1828, several French Canadian servants whose terms of service were about to end and who did not want to return to Canada chose to settle in Oregon. They disliked the Willamette Valley, notwithstanding its fertility, because they thought it ultimately would become American territory and they thought of themselves as Canadian. Doctor John responded that he believed the American government and people acknowledged only two classes of people: rogues and honest men. They punished the first and protected the latter, and it was up to the French Canadians which class they wanted to belong to.

The French Canadians followed his advice. To allow them to become settlers, he kept them on the books of the Hudson's Bay Company as servants, but only if they possessed fifty pounds sterling. He loaned each of them seed and wheat to plant, to be returned from the produce of the farm, and sold implements and supplies at fifty percent advance on London cost. The selling price at Fort Vancouver was eighty percent advance on prime London cost.

Doctor John also loaned each of the settlers two cows on the proviso that any calves they had would belong to the Hudson's Bay Company, as at the time it had only a small herd and he wanted to increase it. If any of the cows died, he did not make the settler pay for the animal. If he had sold the cattle outright, the price would be have been prohibitive since some settlers charged as much as $200 for a single cow. Therefore, to protect the poor settlers against the rich and to make a herd of cattle for the benefit of the whole country, he refused to sell a cow to anyone.

The Methodist contingent was not without its problems. Charles J. Roe was a member of Wyeth's second expedition. He married his first wife, Nancy McKay, in 1837 in a joint ceremony with Jason Lee and Cyrus Shepard. He was considered somewhat of a religious fanatic. He murdered his second wife, Angelica Metisse, in 1859 in a fit of jealous rage and was hanged for his crime.

At that time, the fort hummed with the sounds of industry. The tinsmith fashioned utensils, the blacksmith beat iron into farm tools, coopers shaped casks for furs and salted salmon, and carpenters strained their skills to build seagoing schooners. From early summer until late fall, the tempo of life was strenuous. The annual supply ship arrived from England and goods had to be unloaded, checked, and assigned to outfits. Clerks worked from morning until midnight on accounts, checking and rechecking figures to show that the department had not done too badly for the year. Furs had to be packed and ready when in the fall the ships sailed again for England.

Trapping expeditions had to be readied and sent off. Those returning were welcomed with salutes and cheers. The overland express had to leave on schedule carrying special mail and passengers to Red River, York, Montreal, and even to England. Officers and clerks worked late to send messages to family and friends – inquiries about the progress of children at school, orders for goods and clothing, comments on fellow workers and on company affairs. Doctor John annually reported to George Simpson and the HBC directors. Seventy pounds of paper in a dispatch box containing his messages was carried painfully over portages and the Athabasca Pass each year telling of his hopes, worries, and loneliness on the Columbia.

At its height, Fort Vancouver was the administrative center of a network comprising twenty-four posts, six ships, and more than 600 employees. Senior company staff and their families lived in dormitories and barracks within the palisade, while beyond it to the west was Kanaka Village, home to the lower ranks and their families, as well as numerous natives. By the 1840s, this settlement held an ethnically diverse population, forty percent of whom were Hawaiians working as laborers, along with English, Scots, Irish, French Canadians, Iroquois, Metis, and Hawaiians, and more than thirty different native groups.

Thomas Agonaiska was one of the Iroquois who signed on with the HBC to work west of the Rockies. An experienced canoeist in 1830, he deserted in California. Nonetheless, he was soon back on contract until 1847, when he died at Fort Vancouver during a measles epidemic. His wife Susan died three days later.

By 1836, the products produced at the fort were, in bushels: 8,000 of wheat; 5,500 of barley; 6,000 of oats; 9,000 of peas; 14,000 of potatoes; and large quantities of rutabagas and pumpkins. There were ten acres of apple, pear, and quince trees. The fort's orchards, fields, and pastures stretched for fifteen miles along the Columbia. There were barns, granaries, dairy buildings, a sawmill, a flour mill, and a boathouse. Grazing nearby were more than 1,000 cattle raised from an initial herd of about twenty.

Among other livestock were 700 hogs, 200 sheep, eighty oxen, and 500 horses.

An early guest at Vancouver was Aemelius Simpson, George Simpson's cousin. He always wore kid gloves, and pulling them from his pocket one day discovered some apple seeds that had been presented to him by a lady in London for planting in Oregon.

These were duly put in the ground by the fort's gardener, Robert Bruce, and their seedlings were eagerly watched by Doctor John. When the first apple was picked, it was handed around so we all could taste it. That was the beginning of Oregon's fruit industry.

The interior of the fort was divided into two courts having about forty buildings, all of them wood except for the powder magazine, which was made of brick and stone. In the center facing the main entrance stood the hall in which were the dining room, smoking room, and public sitting room, or bachelors hall. Single men, clerks, strangers, and others lived in the bachelors hall. Artisans and servants were not admitted to these rooms. The hall was the only two-story house in the fort.

Doctor John's residence, the chief factor's house, was built after the model of a French Canadian dwelling. It was one story, weather-boarded, painted white, had a piazza with vines growing on it, and flowerbeds in front. The other buildings consisted of dwellings for officers and their families, a schoolhouse, a retail store, warehouses, and shops.

A short distance from the fort on the banks of the river was the village of more than fifty houses for the mechanics and servants and their families, built in rows to form streets. Here were also the hospital, boathouse and salmon house, and nearby barns, threshing mills, granaries, and dairy buildings. About 800 men, women, and children lived there.

The hall was an oasis in the vast social desert of Oregon, and Fort Vancouver was a fairyland to early travelers after their long journeys. Thomas J. Farnham, a traveler who came to Oregon in 1839, offers a description of dinner at Fort Vancouver:

'The bell rings for dinner; we will now pay a visit to the Hall and its convivialities. At the end of a table, 20 feet in length, stands Governor McLoughlin, directing guests and gentlemen from neighboring posts to their places; and chief traders, traders, the physician, clerks, and farmers slide respectfully to their places, at distances from the governor corresponding to the dignity of their rank in the service. Thanks are given to God, and all are seated. Roast beef and pork, boiled mutton, baked salmon, boiled ham; beets, carrots, turnips, cabbage, and potatoes; and wheaten bread are tastefully distributed over the table among a dinner set of elegant queen's ware, burnished with glittering glasses and decanters of various-colored Italian wines. Course after course goes round and each gentleman in turn vies in diffusing around the board a most generous allowance of viands, wines, and warm fellow feeling. The cloth and wines are removed together, cigars are lighted, and a strolling smoke about the premises, enlivened by a courteous discussion of some mooted point of natural history or politics, closes the ceremonies of the dinner hour at Fort Vancouver'.

William Bruce was a true gardener. Contracted as a laborer for three years by the HBC in 1825, he began work at Fort Vancouver as a gardener. During this time, he was also a stores man and in 1828 was given extra wages on the order of George Simpson. At the end of his contract in March 1838, he left the Columbia and sailed back to England, arriving there in October 1838. After a chance meeting on a crowded street with Doctor John, he begged to be taken back to Fort Vancouver. McLoughlin agreed to send him back on the first available ship, but first he would have to go to Chiswick to gain more knowledge of his duties.

Bruce sailed back on the barque *Vancouver*, bringing plants with him, and began to work once again on the Columbia in October 1839. One of his jobs was ringing the wake-up bell at four a.m. in the summer and eight a.m. in the winter. He died a bachelor at Fort Vancouver.

During the days, my mother taught me to sew and to do beadwork, and we sometimes helped make clothing for people who lived inside the fort. When I was fifteen years old, the first official teacher arrived at Fort Vancouver. Along with other children, I learned reading, writing, math, and took lessons in biblical studies. I also learned to recite poems and passages from books.

3.8

Cecilia Douglas was born in October 1834 at Fort Vancouver to James and Amelia Douglas. They lived in the chief factor's house alongside our family. Amelia did not care for Fort Vancouver very much. She was born at Norway House, a Hudson's Bay Company fort in Manitoba, the daughter of an HBC officer and a native woman, and liked Cree food more than European-style food and preferred the colder weather of her homeland over the warmer summers in Vancouver. She was often sick with fever and ague, or malaria, which was common at Fort Vancouver.

At the chief factor's house, Cecilia and her sisters shared a bedroom. They had beds that folded up against the wall, which gave them room to play. For her eleventh birthday, she and her friends celebrated with a card party and a special supper in the loft. With them was George Stewart Simpson, son of the most important man in the North American fur trade, George Simpson. However, that didn't mean his life was easy. George Stewart was born in 1827 at the Red River settlement in Manitoba. His mother was Margaret Taylor, a Metis woman. When George was very young, his father suddenly abandoned his mother so he could marry his cousin Frances. When George was eight years old, he joined the Hudson's Bay Company as an apprentice and was sent to Fort Vancouver with the 1836 fur brigade. At Fort Vancouver, he lived inside the fort at the chief factor's house and played with the other children of the house, including Cecilia. Unlike the girls, he had a job outside the house beating furs in the fort's store in order to remove bugs and dirt and prepare to them for shipment to England. It was a nasty job, physically demanding, and the fleas often would infest his clothes and bite him mercilessly, leaving itchy sores.

Outside the fort, rows of log houses were laid out. Children played while their native mothers did chores, and orchards, crops, and grazing lands surrounded the fort. At early dawn, the bell was rung for the working parties and soon after all were at work, according to Lt. Charles Wilkes of the American Exploratory Expedition. At eight a.m. the bell rang for breakfast, and men went home or to the dining hall. An hour later, the bell rang again and they were back at work. The same routine was followed for lunch and dinner. Work went on from dawn until dusk six days a week. Vancouver was no place for an idle person, Wilkes noted.

Brigades generally set out in spring from opposite ends of the continent, one from Fort Vancouver laden with furs and the other from York Factory on

Hudson's Bay with supplies, passing each other in the middle of the continent. Each brigade consisted of up to seventy-five men and several specially made boats and traveled at what for the time was breakneck speed. Natives along the way were paid in trade goods to help portage the boats around falls and rapids. An 1839 report cites the travel time as three months and ten days – twenty-six miles a day on average. These men carried supplies in and furs out by boat, horseback, and as backpacks for the forts and trading posts along the route. It was a major celebration welcoming the York Factory contingent to Fort Vancouver each year.

Philip Leget Edwards was a native of Kentucky. In 1834 at age twenty-two, he joined the Jason Lee expedition to Oregon as a lay helper. He taught school at Champoeg in 1835 and in 1836 went to California with other settlers to obtain cattle for the mission. In March 1838, he returned to the United States with Jason Lee. He practiced law in Richmond, Missouri, until 1850, when he traveled overland to California, was elected to the California Legislature, and died at Sacramento.

In 1839, teacher John Fisher Robinson was caught taking sexual liberties with the young daughter of a chief trader, John Work. James Douglas had Fisher tied to one of the cannons in front of the big house during Doctor John's furlough in England, summoned the entire populace to watch, and flogged the culprit mercilessly. The affair so shook the fort that schooling lapsed for a time and was not resumed until 1844 when George Robert's new English bride agreed to tutor the officers' children for £5 a year per pupil.

James Douglas, Doctor John's assistant, was cut in much the same mold as George Simpson. He was born in 1803 in British Guiana. His father, John Douglas, was a Scottish plantation owner and his mother was a Creole woman, Martha Ann Telfer, known as 'Miss Richie'. She was classified as 'free colored', which meant that she was a free person of mixed African and European ancestry. She was probably a mulatto servant on the Douglas plantation. John Douglas' second family were the children of Jessie Hamilton, whom he married in Glasgow in 1809 and who James stayed in touch with.

Placed at an early age in a preparatory school in Scotland, James Douglas learned 'to fight his own way with all sorts of boys, and to get on by dint of whip and spur'. During his early years in the fur trade, he was singled out for having a sound knowledge of the French language and 'possessing a clear and distinct pronunciation'.

James Douglas and his older brother Alexander were apprenticed to the Nor'West Company when James was sixteen. At Fort William, James learned accounting and business methods. In summer 1820, he transferred to Ile-a-la-Crosse and threw himself into the struggle between the Nor'Westers and the Hudson's Bay Company, fighting a duel and engaging in military maneuvers. He was one of four Nor'Westers warned on April 12, 1821, to desist from parading within gunshot of the neighboring HBC post with 'guns, swords, flags, drums, fifes, etc'.

After the companies merged in 1821, HBC employed him as a second-class clerk. In 1822 at age eighteen he was regarded as 'a very sensible young man' and a good trader who could be trusted to take charge that summer of the Island Lake post. During the winter of 1827 at Fort St. James, Douglas decided to retire from the fur trade at the end of his three-year contract, discouraged by the isolation of his life, the lack of companionship and of good books, the hostility of the natives, and the danger of starvation after the salmon run failed. However, on April 27, 1828, according to the custom of the country – confirmed in a Church of England ceremony at Fort Vancouver in 1837 – Douglas took Amelia Connolly, daughter of William Connolly, as his wife.

As the officer responsible in Doctor John's absence for the Columbia headquarters, Douglas sought to elevate moral standards. He entrusted the moral and religious improvement 'of our own little community' to the fort's Church of England chaplain, but his support was withdrawn when the chaplain, the Rev. Herbert Beaver, proved to be a religious fanatic.

In April 1840, he was sent north to Sitka, Alaska, where he was received with 'the most polite attention' by the Russian authorities and where he arranged to take over Fort Stikine under an agreement of 1839 with the Russian American Company. On these missions, Douglas displayed talent as a negotiator. Like Doctor John, he presented a dignified and self-confident appearance. No detail of government policy, business practice, or social value escaped his attention. The officers and men of the Russian American Company lived in what he considered idleness, and the naval officers employed by the company were 'the most unqualified men to manage commercial undertakings', he said. In Spanish California, he found the government arbitrary and the law feebly administered.

At Sitka, Douglas negotiated the boundary between the Russian and British posts and promised to supply articles needed by the Russians. 'Honesty is found to be in all cases ultimately the best policy', he wrote, 'but in our intercourse with our Russian neighbors it will be found so from the first day to the last of our intercourse'.

In August 1841, Douglas welcomed George Simpson to Fort Vancouver in the absence of Doctor John and traveled with him to Sitka to negotiate once more with the Russians. There Simpson arrived at decisions that greatly angered Doctor John. The far northern posts were to be abandoned, he decided, the trading operations of the steamboat *Beaver* were to be expanded, and a new port was to be established at the south end of Vancouver Island. Douglas made a reconnaissance of the tip of Vancouver Island in July 1842, and in March 1843 started the construction of Fort Victoria.

Douglas realized that Doctor John and Simpson were moving toward a complete break in their relations, but he remained loyal to the doctor. He viewed with concern the interest of the United States in ports on the Pacific Coast. 'An American population will never willingly submit to British domination', he wrote Simpson, 'and it would be ruinous and hopeless to enforce obedience on a disaffected people; our government would not attempt it, and the consequence will be the accession of a new state to the union'. If the United States gained an advantage on the coast, 'Every seaport will be converted into a naval arsenal and the Pacific covered with swarms of privateers, to the destruction of British commerce on those seas'.

Doctor John was able to oversee the construction of the projected chain of coastal trading posts. The first, Fort Nass, built by Peter Ogden on the Nass River, was soon renamed Fort Simpson in 1834 and moved to Port Simpson, a better site on the coast. Fort McLoughlin near Bella Bella, established by chief factor Duncan Finlayson, followed in 1833, and in the same year Fort Nisqually near Tacoma, intended as a farming center and depot for coastal shipping, was built by chief trader Archibald McDonald. Doctor John intended to build a post some distance up the Stikine River, the mouth of which was in Russian territory, but when Peter Ogden arrived to build the post he found that the Russians had blocked the river by establishing a fort of their own and by stationing a well-armed brig at its mouth.

The supply ships from London, arriving in the spring, were supposed to engage in coastal trading before sailing for London in the autumn, but wrecks, late arrivals, and drunken and uncooperative captains played havoc with that plan. From these circumstances sprang Doctor John's strong prejudice against ships as opposed to trading posts. Ships, he contended, were expensive to maintain and required crews with special skills, whereas someone was always available who was capable of building a trading post and taking charge of it.

Other lives at the fort included Angelique Carpentier, the daughter of Charles Carpentier. She and her sister were placed in the Methodist Mission school near Salem for a few years after they were left motherless. After leaving the mission, she had a number of lovers. At the time of her murder at the hands of her husband, Charles Roe, the Oregonian reported, 'She had previously lived with a Negro and a Kanaka and had children by both'.

Alanson Beers was born in Connecticut and became a blacksmith with the Methodist missionary reinforcements that arrived on the ship *Diana* in May 1837. He participated in the establishment of the Oregon provisional government and was involved in forming the first military organization. At the end of 1845, he helped lay out the town of Butteville and stayed on to farm after the mission was dissolved. He was the father of six children.

Peter Arthur was chief engineer of the steamer *Beaver*, sailing from England in the hold of another ship and arriving in March 1836. Less than two years later at Fort Simpson, he helped organize the crew's mutiny against William McNeill for his harsh treatment of the *Beaver* crew. He escaped punishment, no doubt due to the essential nature of his job, and in March 1838 even asked for a pay increase.

James Douglas bristled at Arthur's drinking and his inability to punish the engineer. Arthur redeemed himself by moderating his drinking and continuing to work in coastal shipping on the *Beaver* until October 31, 1840, at which point he sailed for England on the barque *Vancouver*.

3.9

Doctor John made his views clear in 1834 when the brig *Nereide* arrived, the intention being that it should remain on the coast and its captain should become head of a marine department. In Doctor John's view, neither the ship nor the department was necessary and he sent the *Nereide* and its captain back to England. In 1827, in what he later came to regard as a misguided moment, he suggested that a steamboat, able to move about regardless of winds and currents, might be useful on the coast. But by the time the *Beaver* arrived in 1836, he looked upon it as an unnecessary and costly extravagance.

Even so, profits from the Columbia District increased steadily, which greatly pleased George Simpson. A London-bound company's ship left Fort Vancouver in 1836 with a cargo of furs worth $380,000 (more than $8 million in today's dollars). That fall, Doctor John received word that Simpson had recommended and the Council of the Northern Department had approved a resolution praising his work and had given him a bonus and salary increase. He appreciated the extra money but valued even more the 'general approbation' of his services.

In November 1835, only a few weeks after the Willamette Valley missionaries had stored away their first harvest, the administration of President Andrew Jackson directed Lieutenant William A. Slacum to proceed to the Columbia to 'obtain all such information, political, statistical, and geographical, as may prove useful or interesting to this government'. Slacum, a navy paymaster, made his way to Guayamas, Mexico, on the eastern coast of the Gulf of California, but could find no vessel headed for Oregon. He eventually caught a ship at La Paz bound for the Sandwich Islands. In Oahu, paying out of his own pocket, he chartered the American-owned *Loriot*, a hermaphrodite brig engaged in the California hide and tallow trade. It landed Slacum at the mouth of the Columbia three days before Christmas 1836. A Chinook in a canoe inquired, 'Is this a King George or Boston ship?'

Doctor John recognized the spy for what he was but nevertheless cooperated and provided the American with the means for ascending the Willamette River, whose settlers Slacum desperately wanted to interview. They included about ten Methodists and forty adult men, half of whom were French Canadians who had once worked for the company.

Slacum offered prospective cattle buyers free passage aboard the *Loriot* as far as the Russian post atBodega Bay in California. Young was elected captain of the venture as an act of appeasement and shares in the venture were sold. Doctor John subscribed to $500 and James Douglas and chief factor Duncan Finlayson pledged $300 between them. Jason Lee put up $600 in mission funds. Ewing announced the dissolution of his fledgling liquor company and then roundly damned Doctor John as a despicable tyrant for forcing him to do it.

In his subsequent memoir, Slacum accused the Bay of inciting natives to attack American trapperseven though Slacum himself was fully aware that this charge was not true. For nearly a decade, Western congressmen would rise to denounce the Hudson's Bay Company as the great murderer of American mountain men and cite William A. Slacum as their authority, a technique that became standard practice in American politics.

The incident with the Rev. Herbert Beaver greatly affected Doctor John. He and Beaver first broke openly over control of the Fort Vancouver school. Beaver accounted himself answerable only to God and the established church. Doctor John was not listed in this chain of command. Beaver therefore included instruction in the Anglican faith as part of the curriculum. Doctor John, pointing out that the parents of a high percentage of the scholars were

Roman Catholic (as he was), Beaver withdrew from the classroom in a huff and refused to conduct services for the burial of a dead child because the child had never been baptized. He refused to baptize another child because she was not in his view properly catechized. He denounced trade or common-law marriages as unlawful and iniquitous. He damned his erstwhile parishioners as villains and Doctor John as the chiefest villain of them all.

Beaver called the frontier culture 'the great moral waste of which I was appointed husbandman'. The Anglican minister was staunchly anti-Catholic and when he took over the school only three or four students out of sixty were Protestants. Doctor John refused to allow him to interfere with Catholic religious instruction, which Beaver ignored. 'The mothers of these children were Indian, and of course from their ignorance of both forms of religion not to be consulted as to either'.

Beaver and his wife found themselves in a land 'where the rifle is the common extinguisher of all animosity'. In official reports, he complained of the food. He found his apartment at the fort inadequate in size and badly furnished. He wanted competent servants to look after his needs and those of his wife. He protested bitterly and repeatedly that his liquor allowance was inadequate for his needs. For months, he and Doctor John communicated only in writing. Just before Doctor John's departure on leave, Beaver handed in a report in which he made an invidious attack on the characters of Marguerite and Doctor John. She had recently entered into a civil marriage performed by James Douglas as justice of the peace with her husband of more than twenty-five years, but Beaver was critical of Marguerite, saying she was 'a female of notoriously loose character'. He also referred to her as 'the kept mistress of the highest personage in your service'.

As a matter of routine, this document crossed Doctor John's desk. He read it and sent for Beaver, who ignored the summons. Doctor John boiled in rage and stormed across the compound. Beaver made way for him to pass but Doctor John 'kicked me several times and struck me repeatedly with his fists on the back of my neck,' then clubbed him with his cane and threw him to the ground exclaiming, 'You scoundrel, I will have your life'.

The following day, Doctor John publicly apologized, much to the amusement of the fort's gentlemen, but Beaver curtly refused to accept the apology and was therefore relieved of his duties. Once Doctor John started for Canada, James Douglas, who succeeded him in command, ordered the chaplain's reinstatement. Herbert was intent on returning to London to bring formal charges against Doctor John and in November he sailed for home. Even the diplomatic Douglas found his patience at an end and in a covering letter he completely demolished

Beaver's catalog of complaints. In the 800 days of his stay at Fort Vancouver, Herbert Beaver was issued 14.25 imperial gallons of brandy, sixty-five imperial gallons of high-proof wine, and 146 imperial gallons of porter. To his last day he wanted more.

4.1

The naturalist John K. Townsend was one of the first Americans to make a scientific study of the Columbia River since the Lewis and Clark Expedition three decades earlier. He studied vegetation and animal life, collecting plants, and shooting birds for his collection. On one occasion, he tried to steal the mummified body of a young girl that rested in a burial canoe suspended in the branches of a tree several miles from Fort William. Under cover of darkness, Townsend stole the body, rolled it up in a reed mat, and hid it in the fort's warehouse. The girl's brother then came to Fort William asking for the body of his sister. Although Townsend had taken off his shoes and socks, the brother 'knew the spoiler to have been a white man by the tracks on the beach, which did not incline inward like those of an Indian'.

The body was returned and the native was given several blankets as compensation. 'The poorIndian took the body of his sister upon his shoulders, and as he walked away grief got the better of his stoicism and the sound of his weeping was heard long after he had entered the forest', Townsend said.

Townsend constantly carried a large two-gallon bottle of whiskey in which he deposited various lizards and snakes, and when he arrived at the Columbia the bottle was almost full of these creatures. He left the bottle behind during a trip to Willamette Falls and when he returned found that the tailor had drank up all the whiskey. He did not discover the theft until it was too late to save the specimens, which were all destroyed.

When the missionaries Jason and Daniel Lee set up their mission, Doctor John loaned them oxen, cattle, and men to drive the cattle, and a boat and crew to transport their supplies down the Willamette River to their site at Campoeg sixty miles from the river's mouth. The missionaries, despite their lofty pronouncements of saving the souls of the natives, arrived just in time to see them so diminished they weren't even sure they were worth saving. Daniel Lee found the natives in a state of ruin following the malaria epidemic. 'These Indians are the most degraded human beings that we have met with in all our journeying, taking them as a whole. They are rapidly wasting away, and the time is not far distant when the last death wail will proclaim their universal extermination'.

During their first year, the Lees cared for fourteen native children, but five died that winter, five ran away, and two more died within a short time. Two years later, only two still remained at the mission.

Many of them said they simply did not want to be saved.

William Slacum spoke openly at public meetings, telling the French-Canadians that 'their pre-emption rights would doubtless be secured them when our government should take took possession of the country'. The only market for their wheat was the Hudson's Bay Company, which paid 50 cents a bushel – in trade goods. The Russians paid $1.50 a bushel in California – in cash. Free trade would have broken the company's monopoly. The company occupied the site of its forts but left a vast area of the country unsettled in order to protect the fur trade. Among settlers in the Willamette Valley, private ownership of land was a critical issue.

This made the missionaries change tactics, and they went from saving the natives to preparing Oregon for annexation to the United States. This kind of tolerance by Doctor John infuriated George Simpson, who hated Americans. No matter where he went, the splendid figure of Doctor John, with his silver mane, flowing cloak, and gold-headed walking stick, was revered by the natives almost to the point of idolatry. This left the diminutive Simpson brewing in anger and envy.

4.2

At this time, Dear Reader, it is necessary for me to enter a personal note if I am to offer a complete history of our days on the Columbia. I, Marie Eloisa McLoughlin, became a favorite at the fort after I was allowed into the company of the gentlemen. I was not allowed to see them until the arrival of Dr. Marcus Whitman and his wife Narcissa in 1836. In her journal, Narcissa Whitman described me at nineteen years of age as 'quite an interesting young lady'. I was of marriageable age by that time and drew the attention of a fur trader, Francis Ermatinger, an HBC clerk with extensive field experience. He began appeals to Doctor John for my hand as early as the winter of 1831-32, describing me as a 'fine girl' who had 'improved much by the company of the ladies from England and America'. His letters indicate a desire to marry into the McLoughlin family in order to further his career and settle down after living the peripatetic life of a fur trader.

After repeated requests, I gave him my final refusal in 1838. Nineteen years my senior, he attributed his failure to the fact that he was too old for me. At the time of that defeat, Ermatinger wrote to his brother that it was clear who my husband was to be – William Glen Rae. I had no hard feelings against Francis Ermatinger and in fact thought him a good man, but I simply did not want to marry him.

William Glen Rae was a clerk who had been stationed at Fort Vancouver in 1837. He was born in 1808 in Orkney, Scotland. His brother John would go on to become one of the most celebrated Arctic explorers of the nineteenth century. William arrived in Canada in 1827, and George Simpson in his Character Book wrote that Rae was 'A very fine high-spirited, well-conducted young man of tolerably good education. Stout, strong and active, he is quite a mechanical genius and can turn his hand to anything. … Rae promises to become a rising man in the country'.

William Glen Rae was quite dashing and closer to my age than Francis Ermatinger, who understood that the nineteen years difference was an impediment to marriage. It was gracious of him to say so, but there was more to it than that, and I leave it to the reader's imagination to discern what it was.

William and I were married in 1938 in a ceremony performed by the Rev. Herbert Beaver. William had earned Beaver's ire since he was one of several HBC employees at the fort who openly sided with Doctor John against him. Of the wedding, Beaver wrote that he wished he had 'united the girl, who is of an amiable disposition and tolerable education', with a 'young man of a milder disposition'.

On February 3, 1839, I gave birth to our first child, John. The witnesses at his baptism a week later included his uncle, John McLoughlin Jr., who by that time had rejoined the family at Fort Vancouver and become an employee of the Hudson's Bay Company. Also in 1839, William was promoted to clerk in charge and sent to Fort Stikine, the rugged outpost in Russian Alaska. I accompanied him along with our baby son. John McLoughlin Jr. also joined us, assigned to the fort as a clerk and surgeon.

Fort Stikine was a miserable place. Only flat rocks with no trees surrounded it in order to better fend off attacks. Within half a mile there was just bare rocks. Alcohol was a prominent part of life at Stikine and was part of the fort's turbulent, destructive atmosphere. Employees were continually buying liquor and fighting among themselves outside the fort's gates. It was a terrible place.

In 1841, William received a new assignment and we boarded the HBC steamship *Beaver* heading south. I was heavily pregnant at the time and gave birth aboard the *Beaver* to a daughter, Margaret Glen, on March 21, 1841. On May 15, we arrived at Fort Vancouver, where Margaret Glen was baptized.

For years Doctor John had resisted the Hudson's Bay Company's desire to set up a post in California.

In 1841, however, he relented and, without consulting HBC officials, sent William Glen Rae to establish a post at Yerba Buena, later renamed San Francisco. With the new position came the title of chief trader. After we had recuperated at Fort Vancouver, I and our two children joined him there. Doctor John assigned William the task of establishing the post without having gotten the explicit support of George Simpson. In 1842, Doctor John and Simpson visited the post, and after leaving, Simpson decided that it should be closed by the end of 1843. Doctor John resisted, insisting that the post eventually would be successful.

Yerba Buena, which means Good Herbs, had a vibrant Spanish community with an openness similar to that of Fort Vancouver. It was almost as sophisticated, but with Spanish mannerisms. While there, I gave birth to our third child, Louisa, in 1843.

My husband was plagued by a host of issues in running the post, including a lack of open lines of communication with the HBC, lack of reliable help, and hostile local authorities. His problems were magnified by his own involvement in contentious local politics and a combination of alcoholism and depression. On January 19, 1845, sad to say, he committed suicide as a result of his troubles. William could not abide by failure in anyone, especially in himself. In the days leading up to the tragedy, I was confined in childbirth. William had discussed fears that he might be attacked by local militants because of his interference in local revolutionary politics and expressed suicidal intentions. I pleaded with him but was ultimately unsuccessful. Shortly after his death, I gave birth to a son, William Glen Rae Jr., who died shortly after. It was a double tragedy for our family.

Not knowing what happened, that March Doctor John sent a ship to Yerba Buena with orders that the post be closed. I returned to Fort Vancouver in June with our three daughters and news of the tragic fate of William Glen Rae. The deteriorating relationship between Doctor John and the Hudson's Bay Company came to a crisis in spring 1845 when his tenure as the head of the Columbia District was terminated. Punitive financial penalties issued by the company at the instigation of Simpson forced Doctor John to return to the home he had built on his land claim in Oregon City near Willamette Falls. We moved into the house with him in early 1846.

4.3

An interesting character during that time was Marcus Whitman, born at Rushville, New York, on September 4, 1802. His father, Beza Whitman, was a tanner and a currier. Shortly after his father's death, when Marcus was eight years old, he went to live with his grandfather, Deacon Samuel Whitman, in Plainfield, Massachusetts, where he studied Latin. He wanted to become a minister, but his three brothers objected so strenuously that he decided to become a doctor instead and studied medicine for three years, receiving his diploma in 1824. Nine years later, he joined the Presbyterian Church, in which he became a ruling elder. In 1838, he joined the Mission Church of Oregon. The American Board of Commissioners for Foreign Missions had sent a missionary from the Sandwich Islands to visit Oregon and report on the prospects, and his report came back favorable. Meanwhile, the Rev. Samuel Parker wrote to the mission board offering to go as a missionary to the natives of Oregon and 'save their souls from the devil'.

Whitman was commissioned to go with Parker, and they left St. Louis in April 1835 for Liberty, Missouri, where they joined the caravan of the American Fur Company. At Green River, Whitman removed an arrowhead from mountain man Jim Bridger that was three inches long and had been shot into his back three years before in a skirmish with Blackfoots. This was before the days of anesthetics, but the fur traders had learned stoicism from the natives and Bridger didn't show any sign of pain during the surgery.

Whitman noted a surgical operation in a wagon train of which he was a member. A herd of buffalo had run through the wagon train, causing the oxen to stampede, and one of the men was thrown from the front seat of his wagon. The loaded wagon passed over him, breaking his leg just above the knee. One of the members of the wagon train who had been a butcher volunteered to cut his leg off, and the man with the broken leg was placed on the ground, his arms and legs were spread out, and three men were detailed to sit on him, one on each arm and one on his uninjured leg. A fire of sagebrush was built and the endgate rod of his wagon was heated until it was cherry red.

The butcher cut off his leg, sawed the bone with a meat saw, seared the bleeding arteries with the red-hot endgate rod, and with a sack needle and some twine sewed the flesh up so the bone didn't project.

Six weeks later, they made some crude crutches for the man and before they reached Oregon he was hobbling around successfully on a peg leg.

Whitman secured additional missionaries including the Rev. H.H. Spalding and his wife, Eliza, in perhaps one of the most disastrous liaisons of all time. The missionary board told Whitman that it would be expedient for him to go as a married man rather than a single man as a missionary to the natives. At Angelica, New York, he was introduced to Narcissa Prentiss, a member of the Congregational Church who had attended Franklin Academy. Before meeting Whitman, she'd written to the mission board asking to be sent as a missionary to the natives. Whitman and Prentiss were married in the church at Angelica in February 1836 the day before their departure for the rendezvous. They barely knew each other.

At Cincinnati, Spalding and his wife joined them. He had been an unsuccessful suitor for Narcissa's hand and never got over her. You can imagine the tension as he shared a wagon with the much more handsome and robust Marcus Whitman.

Whitman purchased for the trip across the plains two wagons, eight mules, twelve horses, and sixteen cows, as well as blacksmith tools, a plow, seeds, and other equipment necessary to start a mission. Although urged by others to abandon his gear, he did not want to leave the equipment behind and stubbornly continued on with the wagons. Narcissa and Eliza were the first two women to make the trip overland to Oregon. On July 4 they entered South Pass. An express rider from the rendezvous at Green River was sent to meet them, and that night a group of Nez Perce and Flatheads arrived to meet them as well, intrigued with the presence of the women.

At the rendezvous, they ran into Nathaniel Wyeth, who had just sold Fort Hall to the Hudson's Bay Company and was on his way back east.

George Adams was one of twenty Kanakas recruited in Hawaii for Nathaniel Wyeth's Columbia River Fishing and Trading Company in 1834. He arrived in the Columbia and set out for Fort Hall in a brigade. Conditions were difficult, with as little as two hours of sleep a night and very little to eat. In November, twelve Hawaiians including George deserted. By October, George had joined the HBC and was trapping on the Snake River. After serving three years, he was discharged and went back to Oahu in 1840.

Practically everyone advised Whitman to leave his wagon at Green River since they thought it would be impossible for him to take the wagon over the Bear River Mountains. However, the natives thought it could be done, so the wagon was cut down to a two-wheeled cart and the extra wheels and the axletree carried on the cart. At Fort Boise, Whitman was informed that the trail over the mountains in many places was a narrow ledge along the edge of a precipice and that if he took the cart it would have to be carried in pieces on their backs. Whitman left it there but determined to come back and retrieve it.

They arrived at Fort Walla Walla on September 2. The HBC factor furnished them with boats and native oarsmen, who took them down the river to Fort Vancouver. Doctor John invited them to make Fort Vancouver their home for as long as they liked.

After two weeks, Whitman, Spalding, and Gray started back up the Columbia to look for a mission site. Whitman and Gray chose The Dalles, but Spalding objected so violently that they yielded to his wish to locate the mission farther inland. Later, the Methodists established a mission at The Dalles, a more promising commercial site.

Doctor John forwarded Whitman's orders for goods to England, accepting drafts on the American Board of Missions, and when the goods arrived saw that they were sent up the river to the missions at Lapwai and Waiilatpu at very little expense. Whitman chose his station at the mouth of Mill Creek about six miles from Walla Walla. It was five days' ride from Walla Walla to Vancouver.

The Nez Perce, among whom Spalding staked his mission, were among the most intelligent, most numerous, and undoubtedly the strongest and most friendly natives in the Pacific Northwest. There were 2,500 of them there in 1836. The Cayuse, among whom Whitman had situated his mission, often intermarried with the Nez Perce and most of them knew the language. Though small in number, consisting of about 300 people, the Cayuse had enormous influence with other tribes since they controlled the gateway to the upper Columbia. They also were some of the most difficult natives in the region to deal with.

Whitman noted as an example of Cayuse thinking a young man who deliberately shot himself through the body in order to prove the strength of his supernatural protecting spirit. The ball entered his abdomen a little to the right and below the umbilicus and came out by an oblique line near the spine on the same side. The third day afterward, he encamped near Whitman's mission for the night. 'I saw him and examined his wound in the morning. He was walking about and making preparations to depart. Soon he rode off on horseback. This was the second trial of his strength, he having shot himself through in much the same way two years before. He will now be regarded as a strong mystery or medicine man'.

Narcissa Whitman was described by a writer as 'a large, stately, fair-skinned woman, with blue eyes and light auburn, almost golden hair. Mrs. Spalding was more delicate than her companion, yet equally earnest and zealous in the cause they had undertaken. The natives would turn their gaze from the dark-eyed, dark-haired Mrs. Spalding to what to them was the more interesting golden hair and blue eyes of Mrs. Whitman, and they seemed to regard them as beings of a superior nature'.

It was extremely difficult for Narcissa to accept the established customs of the native peoples, who already possessed a rudimentary form of Christianity that meshed with their own beliefs. On June 27, 1836, she wrote: 'Dear brother and sister Whitman: The next day, in the morning, we met a large party of Pawnees going to the fort to receive their annuities. They seemed to be very much surprised and pleased to see white females; many of them had never seen any before. They are a noble Indian – large, athletic forms, dignified countenances, bespeaking an immortal existence within'.

On July 16 at Green River: 'As soon as I alighted from my horse I was met by a company of matrons, native women one after the other shaking hands and saluting me with a most hearty kiss. This was unexpected and affected me very much. They gave Sister Spalding the same salutation'.

On July 27: 'Feel to pity the poor Indian women, who are continually traveling in this manner during their lives and know no other comfort. They do all the work and are complete slaves of their husbands. I am making some little progress in their language; long to be able to converse with them about the Saviour'.

On September 11: 'I saw an infant here whose head was in a pressing machine. This was a pitiful sight. Its mother took great satisfaction in unbinding and showing its naked head to us. The child lay upon a board between which and its head was a squirrel skin. On its forehead lay a small square cushion, over which was a bandage drawn tight around, pressing its head against the board. In this position it is kept three or four months or longer until the head becomes a fashionable shape. There are a variety of shapes among them, some being sharper than others. I saw a child about a year old whose head had been recently released from pressure, as I supposed from its looks. All the back part of it was a purple color, as if it had been sadly bruised. We are told that this custom is wearing away very fast. There are only a few tribes in this river who practice it'.

The Methodist Board of Foreign Missions saw opportunity in Oregon as a result of the positive report they had received and approved the dispatch of seventeen additional missionaries, appropriating $30,000 for their travel and support. Unencumbered with a family and eager to live among the natives, preach Christ, and introduce them to the wonders of civilization, the Rev. Jason Lee was considered the ideal candidate for the Oregon mission superintendency. But when Jason Lee met his first natives near Louisville, Kentucky, his psyche never recovered from the shock. He had nothing but revulsion and disgust for them, and the very sight soured his charitable impulses. He was a copper-riveted product of the Protestant work ethic. His reaction to the Caws demonstrated that Lee was constitutionally unable to love the unlovable.

Jason Lee and his nephew Daniel Lee both arrived in 1835. More Methodists came in 1837, followed by two Catholic priests, and three additional Presbyterian missionary couples came the next year. Jason Lee returned by ship in 1840 bringing fifty-one American missionaries, laymen, and their families. Doctor John welcomed them, sheltered them at Fort Vancouver, sometimes for months at a time, and provided them with food, supplies, tools, and transportation to help them settle in.

Another one sent to help the hapless souls was Thomas Jefferson Hubbard, who came to the Oregon country with Nathaniel Wyeth's second expedition in 1834. Shortly after his arrival, he was living with a native woman. Her former lover, a man named Thornburgh, vowed to get her back and broke into their cabin in the dead of night. Hubbard shot and killed him. An inquiry into the murder judged it to be justifiable homicide, and Thomas formally married her in 1837. During the gold rush, he built a ship at Oregon City, loaded it with flour, and sailed it to San Francisco, where he sold both the cargo and vessel and made a fortune.

Then there was Urbain Heroux (pronounced Ero), who was born in Pointe-du-Lac in Lower Canada. At age twenty, he was caught trespassing at a building on a wharf, but his punishment was commuted on the condition that he seek employment outside Lower Canada. He was hired by the Hudson's Bay Company in spring 1833 and sent to several interior posts. In 1837, he was appointed to Fort Vancouver, where he had at least one child with a Chinook woman. From there he served intermittently at Fort Vancouver and Fort Stikine, arriving in 1841. Fort Stikine was in the Stikine lisiere, a territory of Russian America leased to the HBC by the Russian American Company. Among his duties he served as an interpreter.

During his time at Fort Stikine, he was caught stealing alcohol by William Glen Rae and later became embroiled in disputes with Doctor John. These poor relations erupted into a confrontation that ended with John McLoughlin Jr.'s death on April 21, 1842. Several other men later testified that John Jr. was prone to alcoholism and had tried to kill Heroux.

Heroux was released in 1843 due to Russian disinterest in the case and transported by the *Cadboro* and later the *Beaver* to Fort Victoria and Fort Vancouver. From there he went to Norway House. In 1846, authorities in Canada concluded that the expense of shipping Heroux and all the witnesses to the United Kingdom for trial would be exorbitant and the case was closed. Heroux returned to Trois-Rivières.

Elmermach, or Mary Anne, married Alexis Aubichon, a twenty-seven-year veteran fur trader and independent trapper. When Aubichon retired in 1841, the family relocated to French Prairie. There Alexis participated in forming Oregon's provisional government and the Aubichons became successful farmers. They raised a family of eight children and operated a ferry landing and hotel from their home.

Alexis Aubichon spent his younger years traveling and exploring the wilderness and joined Hudson's Bay Company to foster exploration in the west. During the conscription of Napoleon's army in 1791, his family left France and settled in Canada. In 1811, he joined the settlement of the Red River of the North, where he met a native woman. The couple had one son together. Aubichon and his brother were drafted into the British army but were rejected because of their French heritage so they left and joined the American army. After being honorably discharged, they became American citizens. Aubichon joined HBC at the time of the coalition in 1821 and for the next three years was part of the brigade between Montreal and the Columbia. After leaving the service at age fifty in 1841, he settled in the Willamette River Valley a few miles below Champoeg on the river and the boat landing at that location was long known as Obishon's Landing. There he voted against the organization of the provisional government. He was successful at farming and in 1844 owned 270 horses, 1,800 cattle, and 155 hogs.

Elmermach's sister Ec-cle-sic, or Amelia, wed Urbain Heroux, and a son was born in 1840 at Fort Vancouver. A daughter followed in 1841. Ec-cle-sic did not stay married to Heroux for long. In 1842, he became implicated in the murder of John McLoughlin Jr. at Fort Stikine. The murder never went to trial. Still, the HBC sent Heroux to several different posts and ultimately to Canada. In 1844, Ec-cle-sic gave birth to a son by Pierre Durival, and by the time Heroux died in in 1853, Ec-cle-sic and Peter had settled at Pillar Rock to raise their family. Ec-cle-sic eventually gave birth to fourteen children, with Durival acting as stepfather to her first two.

4.4

Doctor John did what he could to confine the missionaries to the Willamette Valley south of the Columbia. He convinced Jason Lee to establish a mission in the valley instead of going north into Flathead or Nez Perce country. Jason Lee was told that any mission established in that country would be difficult to provision, costly to maintain, and dangerously remote from any protection the Bay could offer. Lee therefore chose a site on the east bank of the Willamette sixty miles south of the river's mouth. But the Whitmans could not be dissuaded from settling among the Cayuse at Waiilatpu near Walla Walla, and the Spaldings went farther north to Nez Perce territory in Idaho.

In 1938, Jason Lee decided on a major expansion of missionary activities and went back east to raise funds. Settlers had signed the Oregon Memorial of 1838 asking the United States to take control of the area south of the Columbia River. The signers included ten missionaries, seventeen Americans, and nine French Canadians. Jason Lee carried the document across the country in a little trunk strapped to his horse's saddle, leaving behind his pregnant wife

Anna Maria Lee, not expecting to see her again for another year. 'Our interests are identified with those of the country of our adoption. We flatter ourselves we are the germ of a great state', the memorial read.

Lee left Mission Bottom on March 18, 1838. His son was born on June 21 and both he and Anna Maria died in childbirth. From Fort Vancouver, Douglas dispatched a special express to overtake Lee with the news, and the messenger found Lee at the Shawnee Mission in Kansas at midnight on September 8, 1838. Lee did not return home as expected but continued east, where he spoke to large audiences about the Northwest, an area of growing public interest. Everywhere Jason Lee lectured admirers thronged to hear him. The Oregon Memorial was presented to Congress, but under the Treaty of Joint Occupancy there wasn't much that Congress could do about it.

Lee was advised to remarry – for the sake of the mission, his advisers declared. They didn't want an unmarried man roaming around out there with so many young native women. He followed that advice and called upon a Wilbraham Academy classmate in Newbury, Vermont, who came up with a potential bride: Lucy Thompson, twenty-eight years old, a recent graduate and valedictorian of her class. Lee arranged to meet Thompson at a church gathering in Montpelier in mid-March, where she expressed a keen interest in mission work. Lee visited her family in Barre, Vermont, and he and the ecstatic Lucy were married on July 28, 1839. It was thirteen months after Maria's death in childbirth. Lee and his new wife sailed from New York in 1839 aboard the *Lausanne* with fifty other people.

Jason Lee contended that he was impressed by the number of natives who had been converted, if not to the Gospel of Jesus Christ at least to rudimentary farming, which was more of an economic imperative. He reported that both Whitman and Spalding whipped their natives, which he approved of, and urged his nephew to be firm in enforcing discipline. He acknowledged that some of the Nez Perce and Cayuse had acquired a knowledge of scripture and seemed anxious to be taught more of the Bible. But he wrote, 'The truth is, they are Indians'.

Daniel Lee, one of the first to visit the *Lausanne* when the ship anchored near Fort George in May 1940, found his uncle in a great dither and so full of importance that he did not remain on board while the vessel beat its way upriver to Fort Vancouver. The next day, he was off in a canoe traveling to Mission House as rapidly as possible. His flock was expecting a disconsolate widower still in mourning for the lost Anna Maria. Instead, when they gathered together to welcome him, he produced a copy of the ship's passenger manifest, at the top of which was entered 'The Reverend Jason Lee, and wife, New England Conference'. As a result, Anna Maria became the martyr of Oregon Methodism. Lucy, although she served Jason three times as long and bore his only surviving child, was scarcely mentioned in chronicles of the time.

Wilkes of the American Exploratory Expedition thought Jason Lee was a rather ordinary man who was unfit for his situation. At Mission House, Wilkes was shocked to see expensive farm machinery left out to rust and acres of unharvested wheat left rotting in the fields. At the training school at Mission Mills, he was shown some half-naked louts lounging in the shade as examples of those who had been 'saved'. He was invited to dine, and they fed him well – salmon, pork, potted cheese, hot cakes, and tea – but they smelled bad. And they charged for everything. He found the Methodists slow, vulgar, and unclean. He excepted their women from this condemnation but could not understand how they would put up with it in their husbands.

George Abernathy, an accountant who came out on the *Lausanne* as mission steward, persuaded Jason Lee that the various mission stations could not be adequately supplied from the middle Willamette, arguing that the falls farther north were more centrally located. Not long after, the Island Milling Company was formed, heavily dominated by Methodist missionaries. This was near the eastern shore of the falls where Doctor John had some years before blasted out a millrace.

The Methodists at Mission Bottom, who were desperately overcrowded ever since the arrival of the 1840 reinforcement, carried on with the initial stages of a relocation a dozen miles south to Chemeketa, a broad, fertile plain (now Salem) along the eastern bank of the Willamette River. Jason Lee laid claim to 2,000 prime acres, began building, and shifted supplies and equipment to the new settlement by canoe. However, he and his associates found the task of assembling a gristmill beyond their capacity.

'The stones were set the wrong way and when at work threw out all the wheat'.

Jason Lee expanded at too brisk of a pace. The dwelling houses and the Oregon Institute for white children at the new mission at Chemeketa, the Island Milling Company, and associated mercantile operations at Willamette Falls were in competition with Doctor John, and the outlying stations at Clatsop, The Dalles, and Nisqually on Puget Sound were more than the enterprise could handle. Lee's obligations to the Hudson's Bay Company, compounded at five percent interest, and the board's reluctance or inability to discharge the debt and increase the subsidy, left the mission in a precarious position. With the steady influx of settlers into the Willamette Valley, the native population, which was the mission's supposed reason for existence, declined to near insignificance.

Board secretary Charles Pitman in spring 1842 delivered a scathing review of Lee's superintendency. He accused Lee of financial mismanagement, of failing to file complete and accurate reports of mission operations, and perhaps most seriously of neglecting his spiritual work and undertaking colony building instead. The board, he wrote, lacked the resources to bail Lee out. Overall debt approached $50,000, and fundraising operations were moribund because the Oregon mission could not supply the anticipated stream of spiritually uplifting stories about leading the natives out of eternal darkness of the sort that inspired Methodist constituencies to pony up.

Pitman went on to lay down the law. Lee must 'undertake no business or enterprise which will in the least interfere with your appropriate work'; he should submit detailed reports of mission activities and finances at least once a year; and he must in no circumstances exceed the budget the board set for him. In other words, Lee must no longer pursue the independent economic and political policies that had fostered development in Oregon.

In March 1842, three weeks after giving birth to a girl, Lucy Thompson Lee died, 'fallen victim to the ardors of frontier life', leaving Lee a widower for the second time. Bereaved, despondent, his health beginning to fail, Lee had to confront the reality that missionary colleagues were proving to be men of little faith. He left Oregon for New York with the object of saving the Oregon mission – and himself. The board heard his plea and absolved him of financial wrongdoing but refused to reappoint him as mission superintendent. Lee returned to his native Vermont in the autumn, caught a chill, and died in March 1845.

A compatriot, Joseph L. Meek, did not attend school until he was sixteen years old. Meek knew about hunting and woodcraft, but when his teacher struck him with a rod, Meeker hit the bald-headed teacher over the head with the wooden paddle on which the ABC's were printed and decided that he had all the schooling he needed. In spring 1829, he fell in with William Sublette at St. Louis and enlisted in his company of fur trappers and adventurers. For the next ten years, Meek traveled all over the West, having numerous hairbreadth escapes. In 1838, he married a Nez Perce woman he named Virginia after his native state.

By 1840, most of the beavers were gone and silk hats had come into fashion. Meek was twenty-eight years old and had nothing to show for twelve years of starving, wading in ice-cold streams, and fighting off natives and grizzly bears. When a comrade suggested that they give it up and settle in the Willamette Valley, he agreed. That fall he applied to the Methodist mission for a cow on credit. He was told that he should pray for one. 'All right', he said, 'I'll get down on my knees and pray for half an hour if you will see that my prayer is answered and I get a cow on credit'. They agreed, and Meek, kneeling in the muddy trail, prayed for thirty minutes, then led his cow home.

Meek became one of the most popular men in the valley. At the meeting at Champoeg on May 2, 1843, a motion was made to form a provisional government. It was voted on, but the motion lost. G.W. LeBreton, in doubt as to the vote, made a motion that the meeting should divide, all in favor of such an organization stepping to the right, and those opposed to the left. There was a moment of hesitation, then Meek called out, 'Who's for a divide? All in favor of an organization follow me'. He led off and for a moment it looked like a tie. Then F.X. Matthieu and Etienne Lucier joined the Americans, making the vote fifty-two to fifty in favor of the provisional government. Meek was subsequently elected sheriff, being fearless and possessing a great deal of tact. He arrested moonshiners, broke up bootlegging, took the census, and collected taxes.

4.5

The Methodists were responsible for the provision that barred settlers from holding claims to town properties or other potential manufacturing sites – a thrust at Doctor John's Willamette Falls venture – but exempted the claims of any mission of a religious character, which meant the Methodists were free to carry on with their commercial developments. The final version banned slavery in Oregon and also claimed for the provisional government jurisdiction of the whole of Oregon until the United States took possession of the country, ignoring British claims to any part of the territory. Taken together, the components were a sharp slap at Doctor John.

The missionaries met limited success in converting the natives to Christianity and to farming. A missionary society was organized among the Kalapuyas. 'The object of the society was to induce them to locate on a piece of ground and till the soil, and to assist them in the building of comfortable housing. A man was hired to help them and some efforts were made in order to induce them to work and to help themselves. There was, however, so much apathy among them that after having used various means for a year quite in vain the missionaries abandoned the attempt'.

Daniel Lee in 1840 organized a camp meeting for natives around The Dalles. He estimated that 1,200 natives attended the meeting. A trumpet awoke everyone at sunrise and early morning singing and prayer followed. 'They were called together three or four times a day, the men and women apart, sitting on the ground, sometimes with a mat or bear skin spread beneath them and a blanket or skin or mat over their shoulders'. Lee said they presented a 'dense mass of black heads and sunburnt faces alternating between adults and babes and little children, withered old age and gray heads'. He told them about 'their own duty to obey the word of Christ, never turning again to their former wicked ways'.

At a second camp meeting, a fourth of that number attended, and another meeting in 1841 drew only a few people. 'Some were powerfully reclaimed from their backslidden state', Daniel Lee noted in defense of his efforts. Overall, the so-called missionaries were far more interested in farming and colonizing the territory than in saving the souls of the natives.

When George Simpson reached Fort Vancouver on August 25, 1841, on one of his periodic tours, he was bound for Siberia on a journey around the world. By that time, he was Sir George, having been knighted for his assistance to Arctic exploration and was more autocratic than ever. Of close interest to him were the new forts that James Douglas had located in the Alaska panhandle in spring 1840. One commanded the bleak mouth of the Stikine River, which was practically a McLoughlin family affair. Its first master was Chief Trader William Glen Rae, who in 1838 I had married and accompanied to Stikine along with my older brother John McLoughlin Jr., Rae's chief assistant.

When William Rae was transferred to the company's new outlet on San Francisco Bay, no one was sent to help John Jr. and only he and one other person were left to handle the twenty turbulent Iroquois workers at the desolate post, many of whom were known for their violence. Simpson ignored all evidence to the contrary and reported to the HBC commission that Stikine was in such good shape that he was able to transfer the other officer there, Roderick Finlayson, to another post. On returning to Fort Vancouver in October, he ordered Doctor John to shut down the coastal forts and use the *Beaver* for gathering furs. He further ordered Doctor John to build a new headquarters post at the southern end of Vancouver Island. The orders undercut years of work by Doctor John since Fort Vancouver would be reduced to secondary status. Doctor John had been in the West for two decades, and yet after a six-week tour Simpson waved those years aside as if they didn't count. He hadn't asked Doctor John's opinion before issuing the directives, and a quarrel ensued as they sailed to San Francisco together. Simpson angered Doctor John even more by ordering that post closed as well. By the time they reached Honolulu, where they separated – Simpson going to Siberia and Doctor John returning to the Columbia – they were not on speaking terms. Simpson delivered his final orders in writing. Two years later, the gold rush turned San Francisco into a fabulously rich city and the center of commerce in the Northwest, proving Doctor John's instincts right.

Simpson stopped again at Stikine to find that John McLoughlin Jr. had been murdered by his own men. Simpson knew that Doctor John would demand action unless it appeared to be evident that by reverting to the ways of his youth John Jr. had somehow caused his own demise. Simpson summarized the testimony of the men at the fort, which stated that John Jr. had 'become a slave to licentiousness and dissipation, that his treatment of the people was exceedingly violent and oppressive' and that any English court would consider the killing justifiable homicide. The Russians did nothing about the incident even though the murder had been committed on their territory.

Doctor John's personal investigation revealed a completely different picture. The post was plagued by alcoholism and theft, stolen goods were traded for sexual favors, and John Jr. had prohibited his men from visiting native women at night. 'Sir George took no person to beat evidence against the murderers', Doctor John said. Simpson turned two men over to Russian authorities and sent a third to Fort Vancouver. Doctor John talked to the prisoner, Urbain Heroux, aboard the *Cadboro*. 'He confessed that there had been a plot formed and an agreement signed among all the people of that place to murder the deceased'. All three were released shortly afterward without charges despite the man's confession.

In search of comfort, Doctor John rejoined the Catholic Church. The investigations he launched revealed that his son had conducted himself soberly, a fact that Doctor John poured out in letter after letter to the London committee while he was demanding justice.

By the time the decision was made for HBC to accept the authority of the Oregon Provisional Government, Doctor John was no longer in sole charge of the Columbia District. Although he did not learn of it until later, he had been demoted. He had not closed the San Francisco post as instructed; revenues in the Columbia District were dropping; and Puget's Sound Agricultural Company was not meeting expectations. The HBC committee in London decided to end his special salary of £500 a year as manager of the agricultural company and place the Columbia under a three-man board consisting of Peter Ogden, James Douglas, and Doctor John.

Word of the demotion reached Doctor John in June 1845. Shortly after came news of the disaster in San Francisco. Rae had taken to drinking and also furnished arms to the losing side in one of California's many revolutions. Fearing reprisals, he committed suicide.

Simpson in effect forced Doctor John to resign from the company so he would be free to manage the Willamette Falls property, which Doctor John felt he had been tricked into accepting by Simpson since he could not buy it under the name Hudson's Bay Company as ordered or it would have been confiscated. He built a fine white house on the riverbank near the mills and moved into it with my mother and myself in January 1846. Not long afterward, Doctor John applied for American citizenship. However, hostility toward him persisted as a result of his years as HBC head at Fort Vancouver. Oregon's first territorial delegate to Congress, Samuel Thurston, went so far as to insert into his land bill a clause that deprived Doctor John of his claim at Willamette Falls, although Doctor John was never actually turned out of his house.

When in 1846 the British accepted the American's proposal of the 49th parallel as the boundary between the two countries, James Douglas reorganized the brigade routes from New Caledonia to make them converge at Fort Langley on the lower Fraser River. In 1849, he moved the company's headquarters, shipping depot, and provisioning center across the water to Fort Victoria. Douglas subsequently was chosen governor of that 'real ultima thule of the British empire' which was to be known as British Columbia.

It was difficult for Douglas to reconcile the conflicting interests of governor and HBC official. The only revenue available for public buildings, schools, a church, and roads were from liquor licenses, and HBC was opposed to drinking. Qualified men were in such short supply that Douglas appointed his own brother-in-law as chief justice of the supreme court. In 1856, Douglas was instructed to give up some of his dictatorial powers and establish an assembly for Vancouver Island. He opposed universal suffrage and sincerely believed that people really wanted the ruling classes to make their decisions for them. Property qualifications for membership in the assembly were set so high that only a few landowners were able to qualify.

Pierre Bibeau joined the HBC in 1832 and worked at land posts and coastal shipping. In fall 1834, he was listed as recovering from a broken thighbone and wrist, and in spring 1837 from venereal disease. He did a variety of jobs, including splitting iron to make nails and working at a forge. On April

27, 1842, as one of the ablest men at the post, he was sent to Fort Stikine to bring stability after the murder of John McLoughlin Jr. After retiring, he took free passage from Victoria to London on the *Princess Royal* and from there went to Montreal on another HBC vessel.

George Washington Bush, one of the first black settlers in the region, came to Oregon in 1844 just after racist restrictions had been passed against blacks and settled north of the Columbia to escape Oregon's harsh laws against people with dark skin. One of the most lasting friendships that developed during the Oregon Trail migration of 1844 was between Michael Troutman Simmons and George Bush, who was a much older man. Both came from slave states, but there was no feeling of superiority or inferiority between them. In 1844, a small group of immigrants chose to settle north of the Columbia River, among them Simmons, his wife, and seven children. The Bush family settled near Olympia and established a settlement, Bush Prairie, at the southern tip of Puget Sound. Bush and Simmons built the area's first gristmill and sawmill, and Bush helped finance Simmons' logging company.

Asahel Munger and his wife Eliza were independent missionaries who traveled to the Oregon Country in 1839, where they hoped to settle with a local tribe and become self-sufficient. After arriving in the area, they realized that establishing an independent mission was much harder than they'd envisioned. Munger went to work for Marcus Whitman as a carpenter, and the Mungers stayed at Waiilatpu until spring 1841. Munger was an excellent worker but it became obvious that he was suffering from mania, and Whitman tried to send him, his wife, and infant child to the annual fur trappers rendezvous in the hope that he could be taken to the United States for treatment. However, there was no rendezvous that year and the Mungers went instead to the Willamette, where the Methodists hired him as a smithy. By December, he came to believe that if he died the Lord would raise him to life again within three days. To convince skeptics of his sincerity, he nailed himself to the hearth of his fireplace, managing to pin one hand to the wall before the pain and heat so overcame him that he fell in among the coals. This cured him rapidly of his error but burned him so badly that he died shortly afterward. He did not resurrect in three days as he thought he would.

4.6

James Douglas did not possess Doctor John's sense of justice combined with his paternalism. His attitude toward natives was one of benevolence for the most part, although he followed the HBC rule that outrages must be speedily punished. To hunt a Cowichan murderer in 1853, he organized the Victoria Voltigeurs, a group of HBC volunteer militiamen, enlisted the services of the Royal Navy, and for the trial empaneled a jury on board the *Beaver*.

Needing a substantial number of non-Americans since New Caledonia was populated largely by Americans, Douglas found potential immigrants in San Francisco. Hundreds of free blacks had reached California in the gold rush years but faced the same prejudice and oppression they had known back home. Worse, the 1857 Dred Scott decision made by the U.S. Supreme Court explicitly denied citizenship to all blacks, free or enslaved. San Francisco's black community was actively discussing the idea of emigrating to a more welcoming country, and Douglas promoted his own colony as a destination. In April 1858, he sent the steamer *Commodore* to San

Francisco and invited the blacks to settle in Victoria. They arrived on April 25, and three delegates met Douglas that same day. They found him 'very cheerful and agreeable'. By early summer, hundreds of blacks had arrived in the colony and established themselves. They made bricks, sheared sheep, built houses, and opened businesses from clothing stores to barbershops. Most were Jamaicans, but all were British subjects.

In 1843, the provisional government of Oregon was organized and in July it adopted a law regarding land claims that was spearheaded by the Methodist contingency and aimed directly at Doctor John and the HBC. Doctor John concluded that the only way in which he could hope to protect the company's claims to land at Willamette Falls was to purchase them himself and in March 1845 he sent Simpson bills to the value of £4,173 in payment. George Simpson instantly accepted the bills and they were charged to Doctor John's personal account.

Simpson was well aware that this purchase would force Doctor John's retirement since he would have to move to Oregon City to take personal charge of his mills and properties there, but other steps to procure his retirement had already been taken. In November 1844, HBC secretary Archibald Barclay had written to inform Doctor John that the governor and the committee felt that the advantages they had anticipated from the Columbia being placed in the charge of one person had not been realized lately and that his post of general superintendent and its supplementary salary would end on May 31, 1845.

The company itself was not vindictive and the financial terms of his retirement were generous. After a year of furlough, he was granted leave of absence for two years, and formal retirement was delayed until June 1, 1849. After that he was to receive his full share as a chief factor for another year and a half-share for five years. The bad debts incurred by the immigrants who came over the Oregon Trail were never charged to his account.

In June 1845, the Council of the Northern Department set up a three-man board of management for the Columbia consisting of Doctor John, Ogden, and Douglas. After McLoughlin sent his resignation to Hudson's Bay Company in 1845, he decided on becoming a U.S. citizen and in 1845 consulted with Peter H. Burnett, then chief justice of the provisional government, about taking the oath of allegiance and filling out naturalization papers. Burnett responded that he had no authority in the matter. This gave Doctor John's enemies a chance to say that he was a British subject and had not taken the oath of allegiance nor applied to become a citizen.

On August 14, 1848, the bill establishing the Territory of Oregon became law. On March 2, 1849, Joseph Lane, the first territorial governor of Oregon, arrived at Oregon City. Soon after, the territory was organized and U.S. courts established. On May 30, 1849, Doctor John took the oath and made his declaration to become a citizen as required by the naturalization law.

Doctor John voted at Oregon City in the first general election held there in June 1849, but he did not vote for Thurston as a delegate to Congress, which Thurston found out about. Under the act of Congress organizing Oregon as a territory, all aliens who had declared on oath their intentions to become citizens and taken an oath to support the Constitution and the provisions of the act establishing the territorial government were entitled to vote in that first election. The naturalization law allowed an alien to become a citizen two years after taking the oath and making the declaration if he had lived in the United States for five years. Doctor John officially became a citizen on September 5, 1851.

Doctor John settled into life in Oregon City as one of the most prosperous of its 500 or so residents. He owned two sawmills, a gristmill, a granary, and a foundry. He owned and operated one retail store and had a half-interest in another. In fact, he owned much of the town including the ferry landing. He was generous in donating land for civic purposes, but that did not protect him from envy and censure. Many of the town's residents were living in small log cabins with dirt floors in stark contrast to Doctor John's spacious home. Furthermore, he was a Catholic at a time of anti-Catholic sentiment and his marriage to a woman who was part Cree made him a 'squaw man' in the eyes of his fellow townspeople. Rumors began to circulate and eventually reached Doctor John, who was stunned and immediately wrote a 3,265-word letter of rebuttal.

All these troubles took their toll on Doctor John's health. He had fortitude, but he brooded, with an occasional outburst. He had made expensive improvements on his land claim, including a flour mill and a sawmill, and other buildings. No provisions were ever made by Congress to pay him for the improvements. Even his dwelling house at Oregon City, which for several years had been his home, was taken from him by a section of the Oregon Donation Land Law. He remained in possession of it because the Territory of Oregon did not sell the land, so he was not actually evicted. There was no way to acquire land in Oregon City except by a law passed by the Oregon Legislature. And the legislature did nothing.

Doctor John maintained his kindly attitude to the last. But these matters affected his health and several years before his death he became emaciated, his eyes were deeply sunken, and his great frame stood out, making him look gaunt and grim.

At Oregon City, Doctor John was active as a merchant and mill owner and engaged in an export trade in lumber and other commodities. He was for a short time mayor of the city. The natives still called him Pee-kin, the White Headed Eagle of the Whites.

4.7

As I write this, I can see Doctor John walking along the river bluff outside the house, wondering at the strange vindictiveness of society. He is no longer in sole control of a portion of land bigger than anywhere else in the world outside of Siberia. He is no longer a beneficent dictator who must make instant and lasting decisions that are both fair and lingering. He learned how it was done from some of the best teachers in the world, especially from the great chief Comcomly.

What is truly amazing about Doctor John was that he was able to do it at all. He saw himself as a caretaker, an administrator of a vast empire, beset on all sides by foes who watched his every move and sought his undoing. Doctor John was too careful for that. He had an able adjutant in James Douglas, who saw at once the lay of the land and inserted his own foreboding presence into the equation. Together they made a fearsome duo.

It didn't end well for Doctor John at the Hudson's Bay Company. His fiery temper and bold leadership against the regime of old thinkers and money grubbers in the Bay hierarchy proved to be his undoing. He would not apologize and subordinate himself to George Simpson as ordered and he would not defy the Oregon provisional government as was demanded of him. Instead, he held his course in the face of antagonism and was beholden to the committee but not to the profiteers who milked as much money out of it as they could.

He paid a price for his bravery and adherence to the rules of civility and justice. Yet, Doctor John was never defeated. The race isn't over yet. Long after the likes of George Simpson are forgotten and fur trails across the continent have grown over, after the anonymous beneficiaries of his work have spent their largess and faded away, Doctor John will be remembered as the one who did the near impossible. He did not give in to the temptation of becoming an emperor but as a man who with candor and solemnity created order where there was none.

Doctor John is someone who other people in positions of power must live up to, the one who ruled without allowing corruption to bury him. He became an American citizen because that was the most just way available to him. He may in fact be the *First American*, the one who has shown an entire nation how to conduct itself in a position of power. His legacy has only just begun to be felt.